SOL

In a country where physici[
limb promised lifelong disat
breaks his ankle.

At a time when an illicit sexual relationship was
punishable by death, Naftali falls in love with his half-
sister Tamar.

In a community whose harsh code of conduct meant
almost certain starvation for a transgressor, Rachamim
breaks his vows.

Into the troubled lives of these people comes the
unconditional love of One born to heal and save.

Cover photograph of caves in Qumran by the author

SOLACE

Anandi Saraph

Solace
First published 1997

Typeset and published by John Owen Smith
12 Hillside Close, Headley Down, Hampshire GU35 8BL
Tel/Fax: 01428 712892
E-mail: wordsmith@headley1.demon.co.uk

ISBN 1-873855-26-5

Printed and bound by Antony Rowe Ltd, Bumper's Farm, Chippenham, Wiltshire

For Immanuel

Acknowledgements

Page 13. "Blessed art Thou, Oh Lord," is taken from the Jewish Prayer Book.

Page 19. "My God, my God, why have You forsaken me?" is the first line of Psalm 22.

Page 81. "Yet Thou bringest all the sons of Thy truth," is taken from Dead Sea Scroll, Hymn of Thanksgiving, 7, 12.

Page 82. "I will groan with the zither of lamentation," from Dead Sea Scroll, Thanksgiving Hymn 11, 18.

Page 115. "Thou hast placed me beside a fountain of streams," from Dead Sea Scroll, Thanksgiving Hymn 8, 1.

* * * * *

The historical background of *Solace* is drawn from Josephus, *The Jewish War*, and *The Dead Sea Scrolls in English*, G. Vermes.

The yogic teachings in the book are from the Siddhas to whom I owe an inestimable debt of gratitude for leading me to Yeshua.

My thanks and gratitude to Ann Redmayne for her unfailing help and encouragement.

Anandi Saraph
Bordon, Hampshire, 1997

Chapter One

A small god

Never had earth smelled so sweet from recent rain, never had sun risen on so perfect a day, so special a day, as this the Eve of the Passover. And never had Yedidyah felt so impatient in all his six years.

After so many days of preparation! So many days of enduring his mother's endless sweeping and cleaning; their small house strangely bare as she banished the animals from the room, airing out all the familiar wintery smells. How she had scolded if the children brought inside so much as a single leaf or twig stuck in hair or clothing, how keenly he'd felt her blows when he'd touched utensils set aside for purification. He'd escaped to the roof, where the blankets and cloaks had been spread to dry, consoling himself with the odour of damp wool.

And then at last, with the preparations over, and the promise of the coming Feast, so exciting and different, to have been sent all the way to Bet-Lehem with his brother Reuven, just to bring back Aunt Rivka. It must be Rivka's fault the donkey was so slow, she was weighing him down with her heavy frame and her big bundle of provisions.

"Can't we go any faster?" he fretted, tugging at the donkey's halter.

Reuven whacked the animal's rump, sending the donkey skittering forward on the path, sharp little hooves scattering stones.

"We'll get there in good time," he laughed.

They'd been away two days; an eternity! Two days was too long. He missed Hamoud, he even missed his sister Shoshana, and tonight of all nights, he needed to be home early. For tonight at the Passover feast, he, Yedidyah, would have the honour of asking the four ritual questions. It was his right as the youngest son, and he wanted to be ready for it.

Loosing the donkey's halter, skipping along the winding path, kicking up the stones, Yedidyah chanted the first question in his high child's voice.

"Why is this night different from all other nights?"

He glanced enquiringly at his aunt, sagging solid on the donkey. "Why is this night different? Why?"

Rivka avoided his gaze, suddenly absorbed in studying her swollen ankles poking from beneath the voluminous black robe. He'll find out soon enough, poor lamb, she thought.

The little party rounded yet another curve of the narrow path, and there it was. At last! The village of Bet-Zayit, no more than a small huddle of simple houses ringed by ancient olive trees, hugged the slopes in the shadow of the great city of Jerusalem.

Whooping with pleasure, Yedidyah darted off the path. Scrambling over sun-baked rocks, he snatched up a fistful of small spring flowers and raced homewards, dusty yellow hair flying, torn tunic flapping round sturdy brown legs.

His mother was standing at the entrance to the house.

"Imi, Imi, Shalom we came!" Yedidyah panted, flinging himself at her, butting his head into her belly, where the baby was, smelling the homely smell of her dress, thrusting the flowers into her hands.

"Shalom and blessings," Leah replied, straightening her shawl. "Did you enjoy the visit to Bet- Lehem?"

"It's better at home! Mother I'm off to see the sheep now. I've thought of little else. Did Shoshana look well after Hamoud while I was gone?" He turned to race away, eager to see the beloved pet he had tended since his father entrusted the small lamb to his care. But Leah was too quick catching the boy by the back of his tunic.

"Son, not now. Not now, Yedidyah. Your father will soon be back from prayer, guests are coming for the feast; and just look at you!" She wrinkled her thin nose," What sort of a boy celebrates the Passover so covered in dust? Today you bathe. Surely you hadn't forgotten? I've prepared everything for you at the side of the house. She pushed her son firmly, "Go and see."

"But Mother, the sheep. It won't take long. I'll be back so quickly, you can't…"

"There isn't time now," she said crossly, "Yedidyah, go and bathe."

He forgot some of his disappointment when he saw the bath. His mother had placed a vat of water strewn with herbs, in the sun to warm, and the water glinted, pleasant and inviting. At the side of the vat, on a coarse linen cloth, there was even a small rare cake of soap, made with the costly oil of ripe olives. The child picked it up, sniffing at its lavender scent. And there too, was his new robe, hand-woven by his mother, to wear to the celebration. He glanced around; no one was looking! Shuddering with anticipation at this unusual treat, Yedidyah peeled off his tunic. Shielding his small manhood with his hand, he stuck one tentative foot in the water, then the other, and slowly immersed himself in the bath.

Unaware that a man had crept up and was watching him from behind the gnarled trunk of an olive tree, the boy tested the water. Sprinkling drops on his head, he laughed with delight, scrubbed at his hair with the soap, held his breath, dared to sink his face in the water. Enjoying the feel, exploring the depths, shaking his head so that the long hair flung droplets over the dusty ground, Yedidyah lingered in the bath. The parts of his body usually hidden by his tunic were paler than the rest of him. Clothes change the colour of your body, he thought, admiring the pattern on his foot where the sandal strap had been. He stayed until his skin puckered, then hopped out, dried himself quickly, and wriggled into the scratchy new robe. Perhaps there was still time to visit the sheep, he thought excitedly.

But his mother was back. "Are you ready, Yedidyah? The guests are here waiting to start the celebration. Let me see if you're clean." She scrutinised the young neck, pulling strong fingers through the damp tangles of his hair. The man behind the tree winced, but Yedidyah bore it in silence, hoping he'd make a quicker escape if he kept still; but Leah took him fast by the hand.

"Now come son," she said, "and see the festive table."

Suddenly shy in his new finery, the boy let himself be lead into the house, where he drew in his breath, "Ah!"

The room was so different tonight. Small stone lamps, set in wall recesses, held golden flames. Two candlesticks, tallow candles as yet unlit, stood on the long low board serving as a table. A ritual dish held symbols of slavery and suffering; herbs bitter as the tears of the Hebrew, captives in a strange land, and a paste of fruits, dark as the mud they used, making bricks under the Egyptian sun. There was also a pile of unleavened bread, baked in memory of those who fled with Moses to freedom, snatching up the dough before it had time to rise.

Avinoam, Yedidyah's father beamed at his guests, proud to be welcoming them tonight. Besides his wife's sister Rivka, who came every year from Bet-Lehem, there was the neighbour Daniel, recently widowed, with his pale sickly daughter, Ruhama, and old simple Jacob, eager for the coming feast.

Leah, with her small daughter Shoshana clinging to her skirts moved to light the festive candles, praying with outstretched hands and It was time for the celebration to begin.

Everyone reclined round the table, candle light flickering over listening faces as Avinoam began to recite the Passover story. Yedidyah could picture it quite clearly: the Hebrew slaves wincing under the whip of the overseers; the cries of the Egyptians plagued by the Lord with rivers of blood, with frogs and boils, with darkness; and most awful of all, with the death of their first-born children. But the Angel of Death had spared the Children of Israel and they'd swarmed out of Egypt, carrying that flat bread, carrying their living babies; going towards the desert. Yedidyah was so entranced by the story, he almost forgot it was his turn to ask the questions, until his father gestured to him, and he stood up. With the unfamiliar taste of wine on his tongue, he began; "Why is this night different from all other nights?"

His teacher Naftali had trained his young pupil well, and Yedidyah remembered the other three questions too. "Why, on this night, do we recline, why do we eat unleavened bread, and why the bitter herbs?"

Avinoam had all the answers. The whole life of the family centred around God and His ways, and the ancient stories were handed on from father to son, from generation to generation. The guests Daniel and Jacob were quick to join in, filling the ears of their listeners with stories of miracles and wonders.

The nightmare started when the meal was served.

Frozen in his mind, as in an evil dream, he saw his mother's hand, holding the ladle. An unfamiliar aroma greeted his nostrils as she poured broth, sharp with herbs, into the waiting bowls. He was aware of his sister's hot little hand, insistent fingers tugging at his sleeve, as she mouthed one word, "Hamoud." Slowly, dreadful understanding engulfed him. He got to his feet, clutching at the table covering, upsetting the wine, gaping at the stain on the whiteness. In the long silence which followed, he was aware of the compassion in Ruhama's face, of his father's guilty eyes, of Shoshana shrinking in her festive dress, the other guests staring. Yedidyah's mouth opened, but no sound came as he rushed from the room.

Reaching the lean-to in the courtyard, Yedidyah pulled open the rough barrier with frantic fingers. He knew it! Sheleg, the white sheep, dozed alone. His companion, Hamoud, who was so precious, was gone; those pale pieces of meat in the broth, all that was left of him. Retching, Yedidyah flung himself down close to the remaining sheep, and buried his face in the woolly pelt. Great sobs tore up from his belly, and his feet hammered the earth in impotent rage. All night he lay there; and in the morning, his father came.

Twisting his hands together, he stood in Passover finery, taking in his son's swollen eyes and bedraggled hair.

"It was by the Lord's command, my son," he said at last.

"The Lord told you to kill the lamb? *My* lamb?"

"You heard the story of the Passover. When we were in Egypt, our people were commanded by the Lord to slay a lamb, and smear the blood on the door-post, so the Angel of Death would pass over, and spare our children."

"That was in Egypt; a very long time ago. We are not in Egypt now. It isn't like that now. Why my lamb? You never killed a lamb before, so why now? Why didn't you tell me? You sent me away to Bet-Lehem, so I wouldn't see you kill him. I loved that lamb, and now he's dead."

Avinoam had never justified himself to a child before, but now he said "It's the first time we had enough money for the sacrifice. It's a great honour to obey the Lord's command. Try to understood. It's by the Lord's command," he repeated lamely.

"Then I hate the Lord!" Yedidyah burst out. Avinoam felt a stab of fear. "Son, hush. Never say that again." Relieved to be back in the parental role, he snapped, "Now come to the house and wash. We'll go together to the House of Prayer."

"No!" It was the first time Yedidyah had defied his parent, and Avinoam's compassion died. "You will come," he ordered, gripping the boy's thin wrist.

"No," Yedidyah yelled again, as silently Avinoam dragged him homewards. No child could be allowed to question the authority of a father. His son must obey, even if he had to resort to beating him. His patience was up. It was enough! Sensing this mood in him, Yedidyah let himself be lead, powerless in the face of his father's determination.

The House of Prayer stood a little apart from the village. Built by hard-working inhabitants, it was the villager's pride and joy. Men had sacrificed time and labour to build it, often going hungry as they donated hard-earned coins to pay for its simple furnishings. On this festive day, it was packed. The whole village was there, even the women, safely penned behind a trellis lest they corrupt the men with wanton eyes, and distract from the prayers. Light filtered through latticed windows, illumining thick walls and low roof beams, and a wooden podium round which the men clustered. Wearing a fringed prayer shawl of unbleached wool edged with black stripes, Simon the village elder, face and beard fresh-washed for the occasion stood swaying with emotion, as he recited the story of the Passover, punctuated by fervent shouts of thanksgiving from the worshippers.

In the corner nearest the door, Amnon swayed with a different emotion, eyes darting outside to see if he was coming. What was keeping him, the child with the pale hair? The mother was here, the fat aunt, even the small sister; but the boy and his father were absent. Surely Yedidyah wouldn't miss this meeting? Amnon ached to touch that hair. He'd planned to do it secretly today in the crowded house, but now it appeared the boy wasn't coming.

But no! Here they came at last, father and son, the son quieter than usual, chastened. Amnon studied Yedidyah intensely, shading his face with his prayer shawl. The boy seemed to be muttering something.

From his place beside his father, Yedidyah whispered to God. "I can't forgive You. You had to kill a lamb once, to save the Hebrew children. I think I can understand that. But why do You need to do it every year? This time the Angel of Death didn't come for children; he came for the sheep." He scrubbed at his eyes with his sleeve. "Naftali told me that my name, Yedidyah, means 'Friend of the Lord'. But that's all over now. I can't be Your friend. Not any more; not ever." He waited, frightened by his own boldness, but no mighty arm came through the roof to strike him down. He grew braver. "Are You listening?" No reply. It seemed the Lord was listening only to the sound of people praising Him for what He did so many years ago. Yedidyah lapsed into rebellious silence.

Then he had an idea, startling in its beauty. It was obvious! The God of the House of Prayer was cruel. A needless slayer of lambs. He, Yedidyah, would invent a god for himself, a friend to be with him always; one who would never hurt an innocent sheep. Yedidyah day-dreamed through the long service, and by the time he walked out of the synagogue, he was holding the hand of Eli. His new companion was his own age, and wore a tunic of brown and white stripes. He had curly black hair, large dark eyes, and an amiable disposition. He understood everything Yedidyah said, and would always help him. Eli was to go with him everywhere he went; a god entirely to his liking. As he walked home with the family, he held Eli by the hand.

Amnon, thwarted, watched him go.

"I'm hungry," Yedidyah said quietly to the new friend as they neared the house. "Sit by me to eat, and help me. I'm dreading going back in that room. If you're there, it won't be so bad." Eli understood. It was the first of many meals they were to eat together.

* * * * *

The synagogue reeked of unwashed children. Yedidyah preferred the days he helped his father make pots, but Avinoam, proud that his son was being taught to read and write, insisted he attend school.

The boys sat on the floor in the airless room, which hummed with the interminable drone of prayers. "Blessed art Thou, oh Lord, King of the Universe, who formest light and createst darkness, who makest peace and createst all things," the class chanted. Yedidyah's lips stayed firmly shut. Still angry with the Lord, he longed to be out on the hillside with Sheleg. His blue eyes narrowed as he thought how he'd sit in the fresh air, wind on his face; free. If he could only get out on the hillside, he could find another pretty stone for Ruhama. Lately she'd been too weak to help her father in the house, and now she was forced to sit under that old tree they had in the yard, doing nothing. I'd find her a better stone than the one I brought her yesterday, he mused. Maybe there's still a flower to be found, or perhaps a feather. Yedidyah liked Ruhama; she'd understood about Hamoud. She hadn't eaten even one piece of meat; maybe he could marry her, when she recovered.

Then he saw the ant. Fat and slow-moving, it edged its way along the dirt floor, making for the line of grubby bare feet. Stretching out his big toe, Yedidyah barred its progress, and when the tiny creature started off in the opposite direction, he bent forward and closed his fingers around it. Then, as the prayers hummed on around him, he quickly slid the ant down the neck of the boy beside him, who turned to glare, ringlets tossing.

There was a beam of dusty sunlight coming through the window, and someone had stood in it, blocking out the light. Yedidyah looked up to see the teacher Naftali staring straight at him. He seemed puzzled, dark brows drawing together in the finely sculpted face. Yedidyah tried to look innocent, but Naftali had noticed. With a fleeting gleam of amusement in his eyes, he motioned his disruptive pupil to leave the room, and Yedidyah marched out in triumph. He was free! Naftali wouldn't tell Avinoam. The teacher had been very indulgent lately…almost as if he didn't care what the boys got up to.

Once out of the oven-hot room, the child darted silently home. Arriving at the lean-to, he quickly opened the crude fastening, and Sheleg was out. Then the two made for the hills. "It was stuffy in there, wasn't it, Eli?" Yedidyah chattered. "I'm tired of all those prayers. I'm going to invent my own prayer; one I like. You'll like it too, you'll see."

Amnon, lolling against his favourite olive tree, caught sight of the boy making for the hills. An unexpected treat! His scruffy angel was moving fast, talking to himself, talking to that stupid sheep. It won't be long now, Amnon consoled himself, remembering the women's conversation at the well that morning, how they'd let slip some information he could use to get closer to the boy. Now the sight of the wiry body in the dirty brown tunic, the straight hair glinting in the sun, was working its usual magic. Feeling the familiar ache, he slid his hand under his girdle, moaning. As Yedidyah passed out of sight, Amnon settled back, spent, against the trunk of the tree, to wait for the child's return. He closed his eyes, savouring the sweetness of the coming meeting.

Chapter Two

Naftali

The last of the boys jostled out of the stuffy little room, and at last he was alone. Naftali stepped into the courtyard, inhaling the pungent aroma of the one dusty fig tree as he squatted in its shade, waiting for Miriam, mother of Jonathon, to bring food. So many mothers, all taking time to bring the best they had to offer to this cheat of a teacher. If only they knew, thought Naftali, as in the quiet of the afternoon the thoughts crowded back, buzzing like flies around the ripe fruit of his pain.

He looked up as Miriam approached. Plain face frowning out from under a home-spun head-shawl, she carried a basket covered with a clean napkin.

"Shalom, teacher Naftali," she said.

"Peace and blessings," Naftali answered, waiting for her to set down the basket. But Miriam hesitated. He could see she wanted to talk, so why didn't she begin? "Is there something you'd like to tell me, Mother,?"

She nodded.

"Well?"

A long pause, while she searched for words. Then she said contemptuously, "I saw Amnon this morning."

"I don't know any Amnon."

"The son of Mordechai. A grown man, and an idle one."

Naftali had known from the start that this conversation was hard for Miriam. The village women seldom spoke to men other than their husbands, but now the peasant face showed disgust as well as confusion, as she stood clutching the basket.

"Yes, do go on Mother," he encouraged.

"He was watching a child."

"Which child?" It was like drawing water from a dried-out well, he thought impatiently.

"The potter's son. The one with the pale hair. He was going home from school…"

"And so?"

"Amnon was watching him…and spilling his seed at the same time," she managed in a rush.

"Why do you tell me this?"

15

"Because I'm afraid for the child. And for all the boys. I can't bring myself to talk of such things even to my own Jonathan, and certainly not to that boy's father. You're the teacher; perhaps you can talk to all the boys? Tell them what happens to children who have dealings with Amnon, and others like him."

Naftali knew about the abomination Miriam was hinting at, but it startled him to realise it could go on amongst his own people. He'd thought these things only common amongst the heathen Romans or Greeks. His lip curled. "I'll tell them," he said.

Miriam nodded, obviously relieved. Setting down the basket, she took the pottery jug, and poured water over Naftali's outstretched hands, the droplets falling from his fingers to the dust as he intoned the ritual prayer of thanksgiving over food. He watched until the broad straight back disappeared behind the wall of the courtyard, then looked without appetite at the food. How could he eat with the unpleasantness of his coming task adding a fresh trouble to his mind? But there was bread, made of barley flour, freshly baked, and speckled with dried herbs and seeds, there was a small tangy lump of goat's cheese, and parcelled in clean fig leaves, three perfect dates, plump with the promise of sweetness. Naftali broke off a piece of bread. After the first few bites, he began to relish the savoury sharpness of cheese, the sun-kissed ripeness of dates. For this he could easily thank the Lord from his heart he reflected sadly. Why was it he was so easily pleased with earthly things like food, and yet found no joy in prayer and contemplation? Where had his joy gone? This miserable state of affairs had been going on far too long. What was the point of remaining celibate, and dedicating his life to a God for whom he now felt nothing? Who no longer even appeared to exist? Where had the devotion gone, he asked himself endlessly. Would he ever again feel the blissful rush of a love so strong it spilled over in grateful tears? Perhaps he should have married, he thought. At least then he would have pleased the family and the unsuspecting villagers, all waiting for an invitation to the teacher's wedding. Who ever heard of an unmarried teacher? Better no teacher at all, than one who broke the Law by staying celibate.

He finished his meal, and went back into the inner room to rest. The small sound of branches tapping against the wall, the sleepy drone of insects, the afternoon chorus of drowsy birds soon worked their magic, and he slept.

* * * * *

The sun was still blazing bright when Naftali woke. He pulled on strong leather sandals, and set off for home, with the afternoon breeze playing in his hair, and moulding the thin cotton robe to his body. In order to avoid the crowded trade route which stretched all the way from Egypt to Jerusalem, he took a little-used path, bordered by boulders of white rock that gave off the heat of the sun. He walked steadily until the massive crenellated walls of Jerusalem loomed in front of him, outlined against the deep blue Judaean sky. Naftali's pulse quickened. No matter how many times he came and went from this city of many gates, it never failed to enchant him. He loved its very stones, whose colours glowed rose or gold in the sun, while remaining solidly grey in the shade. Naftali went towards the Gate of the Essenes, and joined the flow of traffic passing through. Some on foot, some on donkeys or camels, people were returning to the walled city before nightfall.

The streets leading to his father's house were crowded with noisy labourers returning home from the grand reconstruction work on the Temple. Absorbed in thought, Naftali didn't immediately hear someone calling his name, and Joseph had to call several times before he recognised him.

"Joseph! Oh blessed be he who returns." Naftali hurried towards his smiling friend, hugging him warmly. "I didn't expect you back so soon."

"Soon? It's been three lonely months. You don't know how much I've missed you. But at last I'm back, I'm well, and thank the Lord, the trip was successful. I was on my way to see you. There's so much to tell. But first I've got to settle my account with the leader of the caravan. Shall we eat together tonight? Say you can."

"I can and I will, for I've missed you too. Come to my house later, we'll go to the Inn. I've just got back from teaching in Bet-Zayit, and need to bathe first."

A party of worshippers filed past on their way to the Temple, and Joseph put his arm round Naftali's shoulders drawing him to the side of the street.

"I saw your face as you came towards me. You seemed troubled."

Naftali felt relief that here at last was a friend to whom he could unburden himself. "I'll tell you tonight," he promised.

But Joseph persisted. "Is it your father? Is he well? And his concubine, and little Tamar?"

"Tamar is not so little, Joseph, you've not seen her lately. And Rachel's no longer a concubine. Didn't Sarah tell you? Father married Rachel soon after you left for India. Now he's away, trading in Greece, and Rachel has taken Tamar to visit the tombs of the Patriarchs in Hebron. I'm all alone in the house."

"Can it be you are lonely, and this is the cause of the sad face?" Joseph teased.

Naftali ignored him. "It's true the house is silent without Tamar, but that's not a cause for sadness. Besides, they'll return in the month of Ellul, for the feast days."

"Tell me all about it later," Joseph said kindly, as they parted with another embrace.

Naftali walked the short distance to his home through hot dusty streets, and was greeted by a smiling servant as he went in at the arched doorway.

"Blessed be he who comes," said Noam, bending to take off Naftali's sandals, and wash his feet.

But Naftali waved his servant away, needing to be alone. "Please tell Abigail I'll be dining with Master Joseph tonight, so I won't need a meal. She should rest today, and I'll see her tomorrow."

On bare feet, Naftali crossed the fine mosaic floor of the inner courtyard, and went to bathe. The house boasted a tiled bath- room as well as the mikvah, a bath used for ritual purification. Naftali chose the mikvah. Stepping out of his robe, he washed hands and feet in a shallow pool specially constructed for the purpose, then went down the three deep steps leading to the bath and immersed himself gratefully in cool running water. But even as he prayed, he was painfully aware of an unusual feeling of sensuous delight. He struggled with it, trying to focus on the prayer, hurrying through the ritual in a vain effort to force forbidden feelings from his mind. He knew Joseph would be coming soon, wanting to visit the House of Prayer before going to the Inn, but Naftali was in no hurry to pray. God was buried somewhere in the tomb of his heart, and the absence of that special sense of His Presence made Naftali feel more like a mourner than a worshipper.

He left the mikvah, dressed in a clean robe, and sat to wait for Joseph on a couch of fine wood, intricately carved, covered with rich brocade. Sitting listening to the silence the familiar emptiness rose again and he sighed, thinking of his half-sister. When Tamar was there the place echoed with her laughter, the tinkling of her silver anklets, the jingle of her bracelets, her voice with the music of India. In the two years since their father had brought her from India with her mother Rachel, Naftali had grown to love his little half sister. Somehow her presence in the house had helped ease the pain of his own mother's death, and the resentment he felt at his father's speedy re-marriage to his moody concubine.

Telling himself he wanted to see if small Yael, granddaughter of Abigail and Noam had fed and watered the tiny singing birds his sister had entrusted to her care, Naftali got up and went in the direction of Tamar's room.

It was a spacious house. Naftali's father, a wealthy glass merchant, had built it in Roman style. Comfortable rooms lead off the central courtyard, each with a door leading to an adjoining terrace. Tamar's room was near the stairs leading to the roof garden. Naftali had never been in her room before, but now he stepped in, looking for the cage. Perhaps Yael had put it in the garden? He went back to the courtyard, and returned with a lighted lamp. Holding it high, he inspected the room. A narrow bed, a chest, a low table. The birds forgotten, he went over to the table, where a fine glass bottle, pale as first grapes, glinted in the lamplight. Carefully he picked it up, and removed the stopper. Bitter-sweet perfume filled his nostrils, evoking memories of Tamar. Replacing the bottle, Naftali ran a finger delicately over a box inlaid with ivory. His father had been generous with his only daughter. Naftali lifted a fine gold chain, hung with leaves made of beaten gold, to grace a slender brown neck. To circle the fragile wrists were bracelets of silver, set with red and blue precious stones. On the bed, Tamar's sweet-box nested on a heap of silken cushions. He picked up a cushion, cradling it to his cheek. Its softness gave off the lingering fragrance of rich black hair. A wave of emotion welled in his chest, surprising him, and he replaced it quickly. Her sweet-box rattled when he shook it. Inside was a single sweetmeat, half eaten, bearing the imprint of small even teeth. Smiling to himself, Naftali raised the lid of the cedar chest at the foot of the bed. Tamar's clothes were thrown in with careless abandon, a tangle of silks and cottons, smelling of frankincense. Naftali stood quietly, wanting to touch, then he closed the lid, and left the room.

* * * * *

By the time Joseph and Naftali reached the synagogue, the evening prayers were nearly over, the congregation intoning a Psalm of David. Naftali stole a glance at Joseph, who had wrapped his white prayer shawl closely around his robe. Joseph's body swayed rhythmically as he prayed, eyes closed, black beard bobbing. Words from another psalm rose unbidden in Naftali's mind. "My God, my God, why have You forsaken me?" To his dismay, he felt tears starting in his eyes.

He tried to force his attention on the rabbi's voice as he lead the worship, but it was no use. Thoughts rattled and clattered in his head, like seeds in a dry pod, and he was relieved when the service was over, and he and Joseph could walk out into the starry night.

The Inn they favoured was in the Upper City. It was a long walk, but the food there was good, and the high location ideal, cooled as it was by enjoyable breezes. They walked towards the Temple, and as the massive outer walls of the compound towered into sight, Naftali said, "I watched you at prayer." Joseph, puzzled, waited for him to go on.

"And I felt jealous," Naftali finished.

"You felt jealous? Of me? But I thought we were friends. Haven't we always been together since we were little? What have I got that you lack?"

"Devotion," said Naftali promptly. "The love of God that you feel."

Joseph stopped to look curiously at his friend. "You have the same devotion."

Naftali shook his head slowly. "No, Joseph, it's gone. Now all I can only remember is how it used to feel, loving the Lord. That feeling of love and connectedness. Oh, that was so precious. To remember only makes it worse."

"How long has this been going on? Before I left for India you were still talking about remaining celibate to devote your life to God. Did something happen to make you change your mind?"

"Nothing happened. It's quite recent. I suddenly felt dry as the desert. The barren desert. I teach the children, I go through the motions of prayer and purification, but it's not from the heart. Can you understand how that feels?"

Joseph put a brown-sleeved arm round Naftali's shoulders. "I need to think," he said.

They walked on in silence, passing through the Hulda Gate into the outer precincts of the Temple, where an arcade of shops, brightly lit, hummed with activity. Sightseers from Rome, eager to see this far-flung province and its strange inhabitants, paraded through the colonnaded street, amusing themselves by gaping at the antics of a people who abhorred statues, and worshipped a God you couldn't even see! Naftali and Joseph crossed the causeway into the Upper City, each still wrapped in thought, and came to the crowded Inn, where the Innkeeper greeted them warmly, and found them a table in the courtyard.

Vines drooped with clusters of grapes, and a cricket shrilled loudly from a nearby tree. A pomegranate bore perfect small fruit, as yet unripe, but still bearing the distinctive crown.

"A prince of fruit," said Joseph, cupping one in his hand. Naftali toyed with the grape juice, waiting for Joseph to speak again.

"Just slightly fermented, perfect," Joseph said, sipping gratefully as the serving girl set down bowls of steaming lentil broth, cucumbers, shiny black olives, and flat white bread. Together they recited the blessings over food, and started to eat.

"Separation," Joseph said at last, picking up bread and dividing it. "Is it a sense of separation you experience?"

"Yes, yes, that!"

"While I was in India, I visited Varanasi. I was determined to question one of those holy men, I'd heard of. Sages who spend their lives in prayer, and claim true knowledge of God."

"Did you find one?"

"Yes. The one reputed to be most famous for his wisdom. It was easy to approach him, but when I wanted to question him, he kept silent. Just went on sitting there on the ground, with his eyes closed, so I couldn't get a single word out of him that first day. One of his followers told me the sage often spends many days, even weeks, in complete silence, so I wasn't surprised it was the same the next day. I doubt he even realised I was there, and I was starting to want to come home; I'd finished my trading, the heat was intense, and the food much too fiery for me. So I decided to try one more day only, and that's when he spoke."

"What did he say?"

"'God is all-pervasive.'"

"Something you already knew."

"Yes. But I'd never really considered what it meant. And then, Naftali, as I sat with the sage, I started to experienced it!"

"You experienced the all-pervasiveness of God? Actually *felt* it?" Naftali leaned across the table, searching Joseph's face. "How was the feeling? Can you describe it?"

"I'll try." Joseph shut his eyes and concentrated, "All I can tell you is God was there. At first I felt Him to be in the heavens, then in the depth of the river. I can't describe the sensation, but it felt familiar and natural, a sort of knowing. How long I sat there I don't know, but after a while I began to feel God was inside all the people, and then most amazing of all, He was right inside of me too. There was no room for anything else. He was All."

Joseph opened his eyes, and Naftali saw they were wet with emotion. "I felt love, indescribable love. And there was nothing else."

Naftali was speechless. They sat in silence, each busy with his thoughts. Finally Naftali asked, "Do you still feel it Joseph?"

"No, alas, not with the same intensity. But I know it's the truth. All is God. There really *is* no separation.

"So if there is none, why can't we all have the experience? All the time?"

"That's exactly what I asked the yogi the next day."

"What did he say?"

"He said 'Maya'."

"What does it mean?"

"Illusion, I believe."

"Illusion? Magic?"

"It seems Maya is a force that veils the truth. Because of Maya, we can't perceive it."

"The veil was lifted for you though. Did you ask how?"

"Of course. But he didn't answer. So I asked how I could regain that experience. And you know what he said? He said, 'A still mind perceives the truth.' Then he was silent again, and I had to leave."

Naftali drummed pensively on the table. "Lately, when I try to pray, many thoughts come. They're like uninvited guests that I can't stop entertaining."

"Perhaps when they take their leave, you'll feel love again. Isn't it the same for all of us? When you thought I was so devoted at prayer, I was thinking of my journey, of how I'm glad to be back safely, of how much love I feel for you, and indeed of all the blessings in my life."

"But what am I to do, Joseph? Do I have to go to India to get back my devotion? What should I do about this emptiness?"

"I don't think you need go to India. The Lord must be here too. Perhaps go on praising Him. Aren't you thankful for blessings?" He waved a hand over the remains of the meal. "For myself, when I feel grateful, I feel love."

It seemed much too simple, but as they walked home under the stars, Naftali felt euphoric, and decided it was because of Joseph's warm concern.

In the house, he didn't go to his room. Instead he went to Tamar's bed and stretched out upon it. Before going to sleep, he took the half eaten sweetmeat from her box, and ate it slowly.

Chapter Three

The Healers

Through the red glare behind closed eyelids, Yedidyah was aware of something nudging his side. He could hear moaning. It seemed to be coming from somewhere deep inside him. Where was he? Cautiously he stretched out an arm, and his fingers encountered rough wool. Sheleg! Yedidyah opened his eyes, then shut them again quickly, dazzled by light. He lay still for a while, trying to understand. His head hurt. He struggled painfully to a sitting position to look around, propping himself on one elbow. Above, the sky arched a fierce blue canopy, and in front, a familiar outcrop of sun-baked rock offered shade. His secret hiding place! He remembered then. He had been nearly there when he'd stumbled. He must have fallen. He tried to get up, but a searing pain came from his ankle. Slumping back to the ground as a wave of nausea engulfed him, he was forced to wait until it receded. As he tried to sit again, driblets of cold sweat sprang out on his brow, but at last he managed to struggle up. Fearfully, he inspected his foot. A large, shiny swelling, big as a small gourd, had appeared there, pain growling dully inside. Fear of moving made him feel sick again. If he moved he might disturb the pain, make it roar afresh. The goat-skin he always carried was still at his waist, and he drank a little stale water. Unwinding his headcloth he wetted it and tried to wrap it round his ankle. It took a long time because of the pain and nausea, but eventually he succeeded. Yedidyah pondered his situation. He was clearly unable to walk. Should he slide on his backside? But the ground was rough, strewn with boulders and the brittle ghosts of thorny vegetation. "What shall I do Eli?" he groaned. "Sheleg what shall I do?" Sheleg chewed the cud peacefully, uncomprehending. Nobody knows I'm here, thought Yedidyah miserably. They won't notice I'm missing. Mother will think I'm visiting Ruhama after school, and by the time she comes looking for me , it'll be dark. He shuddered remembering how quickly it got dark once the sun had gone down. His stomach contracted at the thought of spending a night alone on the hillside. There were wolves in the hills, hungry for sheep. He didn't know if they ate children too, but a tiger certainly would. A tiger had sharp claws. Its breath would stink as it opened its jaws, showing rows of frightful teeth. Yedidyah started to cry.

"Oh God," he sobbed, "Help me. Please stretch out a strong arm. Please help. I need You. I don't want to die."

In his pain he forgot he wasn't going to talk to God ever again. It made sense to ask Him now. He doubted whether Eli could be of much use in this emergency. Yedidyah settled himself uncomfortably to wait for an answer to his prayer, not at all sure it would come.

He didn't know how long he had lain there. Ages seemed to pass. The only sounds were birds wheeling overhead, uttering cries, going to their resting places for the night. Already the sun was a huge orange, sinking fast. A tear trickled down his cheek. "Please hurry, God," he shivered.

* * * * *

Amnon had woken, hot uncomfortable and hungry, from a troubled sleep. He'd dreamed he was walking with Yedidyah, but somehow it was a painful journey, not like the one he'd planned. He hurried home to get food, keeping his eye on the path by which the boy would return. Stuffing bread and olives into his pouch, he scuttled back to his post. But as the slow afternoon wore on, Amnon felt cheated. The boy must be asleep, he decided, and if he sleeps much longer, his mother will go looking for him. Then I'll never be able to persuade him to trust me. But as he waited, and Yedidyah still hadn't returned, he felt a stirring of genuine concern. Something must have happened to the child. Perhaps he'd fallen into a crevice, perhaps he was lost. Amnon's agitation grew. Impossible to sit and wait any longer. Selecting a strong stick, he set out, going quickly up the path the boy had taken. His keen black eyes scanned the barren hills, and his voice grew hoarse, calling Yedidyah by name. Nothing. Only a mocking echo. Soon it would be dark, and he'd have to return, for he had brought no flare.

When Sheleg bleated, Yedidyah looked around fearfully. "Oh, God, don't let it be a wolf. Make it go away. I'll forgive You for killing sheep. I'll say prayers. I'll never say I hate You again." Sheleg was bleating excitedly now, and Yedidyah picked up a pointed rock, holding it ready to defend himself. But it was no wolf. It was that man from his village. Yedidyah let out a gasp of relief, and dropped the stone.

"What happened to you?"

"I fell and can't walk. It hurts me so much."

Amnon unwrapped the cloth, and studied the ankle. He could see from the unnatural angle of the foot that it was probably broken.

Hugely swollen, it pulsed with heat under his fingers. The boy could be crippled for life.

"Can you move it?"

Yedidyah shook his head, faint with pain.

"Perhaps it isn't broken," Amnon lied. "Come, I'll carry you."

Yedidyah held out his arms, and Amnon gathered him up. His rough brown tunic smelled of sweat, wonderfully reassuring to a frightened child. Amnon draped Yedidyah over muscular shoulders, and started the descent, the sheep following.

It was almost dark, the moon a pale fish netted by stars, when Sheleg bleated, and was answered by a chorus of sheep voices. Amnon turned. That blundering shepherd, Boaz, was leading his flock home from pasture. "Wait," the shepherd ordered, stretching out his arms, "I'll take him."

Reluctantly Amnon relinquished his burden, but not before he had passed a hand over the child's wonderful hair.

* * * * *

Standing in the doorway, waiting for her husband's return, Miriam was surprised to see him carrying a child. As she hurried to greet him, one glance at Boaz' grim face and Yedidyah's flushed tear-stained one confirmed her fears. Here was serious trouble indeed. She held out her arms for Yedidyah, "Come, my lamb, let me help you. We'll call your mother," she comforted.

Setting Yedidyah down on a mat in the house, Miriam shouted to her son, "Jonathon, go quickly to the Mother of Yedidyah. Tell her to come." Plump, rosy-cheeked Jonathon detached himself reluctantly from the game of mill-stones he was playing with a group of other boys.

"Naftali sent him out of the House of Study," he said.

"I know. I saw him go," said Miriam. Could it be that Amnon had hurt the child?. "Hurry, Jonathon, do," she urged.

Yedidyah could only give her a garbled explanation of what had happened, mumbling something about falling and wolves. He seemed to be talking to Eli, whoever that was. She fetched water to bathe the boy's fevered face, blanching when she saw the foot.

"I'll make a poultice of comfrey for the swelling," she told Boaz.

"We have no comfrey, Miriam. I used the last of it to heal that ulcer on old Shimon's leg. But I know where I can get some." He ran out, not even stopping to quench his thirst.

In the courtyards of their homes, the villagers were preparing the evening meal. Cooking fires crackled, blackened pots steamed and bubbled, fragrant food smells mingled with the acrid scent of smoke. The alleyway outside the house where Ruhama lived was crowded with people. "Why all these people? What has happened?" Boaz asked, attempting to push through.

"The Essene Brothers are in the village."

"Why's that?"

Daniel fetched them. He's desperate. Ruhama is so sick. He wants them to try to heal her."

"Nothing can heal that sickly girl," a neighbour grunted, "she has the same wasting sickness her mother died of. Better to let her die in peace."

Boaz had no interest in Ruhama, but he'd heard of the Essene healers. Might they not be able to help Yedidyah? He rushed off, nearly colliding with Reuven on his way to collect the child.

"Bring the boy here," Boaz said. It would do no harm to ask the healers their help for the lad too."

* * * * *

Yedidyah screwed up his eyes as Reuven carried him into the room. Through the fog of pungent smoke coming from burning herbs, he could barely make out Ruhama. He forgot his pain for a moment as he strained to see her. She was lying on a mat in the centre of the room, eyes glittering in her thin white face. She'd recognised him, but she wasn't raising her head in greeting. She must be very ill, Yedidyah thought, even worse than me.

Reuven laid him down in a corner of the smoky room, and Yedidyah saw three men and a boy, sitting cross-legged on the ground near Ruhama. They all wore white robes with broad white girdles, their long hair flowing down their backs. They were chanting what seemed to be a sort of prayer, though Yedidyah couldn't understand the words. Then the boy got up, still singing, his thready voice weaving in and out of the fabric of the chant, and came and sat by Yedidyah. Fascinated by the strange sound, Yedidyah gave himself up to the music, which seemed to cover his body like a prayer shawl, taming the pain.

As the chant faded, Yedidyah could see the pale shapes of the three men, bending over Ruhama, their hands outstretched. The hands moved in unison in the air, not touching, but changing places in a sort of slow dance over the unmoving girl.

When the Brothers came to stand near him, Yedidyah tried to make out their faces in the ill-lit room, but as they began to move their hands over him, he closed his eyes, drawn down into a warm light. The light seemed to start in his chest, till spreading through his body, it reached to his toes. Then he was right inside the light; but he wasn't afraid. Instead, there was a feeling of intense well-being, an almost unbearable sweetness. The pain in his ankle was still there; hot, throbbing, and insistent, but it didn't seem to belong to him—he was somewhere apart from it, cocooned in peace.

Hands of infinite tenderness were pulling at his foot, coaxing it, cooling the flames. Yedidyah floated far away, a leaf on water, dancing to the melody that had started again. Sound entered his body, filling it so full there was no room for him, and he became the sound, which swirled and eddied in a rich cadenza.

Amnon, waiting outside the house, had never heard such sounds. They roused an unfamiliar yearning in him, that had nothing to do with the child. There was something here he had to get nearer to. Edging up to the narrow doorway, he peered inside. Through the pale glimmer of lamp-light swirling with incense, he could see three men, sitting near a slight figure on the ground. That must be the boy, he thought with a pang, wanting to go to him. He tried to get in, but the man at the door barred his way, holding a finger to his lips for silence, and Amnon was forced to retreat. He didn't go far, but hovered near the doorway, hoping the singing would start again, longing to be near the strangers with the haunting voices which had sparked the unfamiliar feelings in him. When he could bear it no longer, he crept back to the door, but the doorman again barred the way. Exasperated, Amnon groaned aloud, and one of the Brothers looked up and saw him. He nodded permission, and Amnon sidled in quickly, and sat near the wall. To his surprise, tears started in his eyes as he sat, and he didn't try to stop them, letting them flow unchecked.

The young boy was holding a cup to Yedidyah's lips, encouraging him to drink. The herbal drink was cool and sweet, and Yedidyah drank thirstily.

"You must rest on your bed for some days," the boy said, "and take the medicine we give you. If you do as you're told, your foot will be quite healed."

"What's your name?" Yedidyah asked.

"I'm Ezra."

"Do you help them?" Yedidyah gestured towards the Brothers.

"I help a little. I'm their apprentice. They teach me."

"I, too, have a teacher, but he doesn't teach me to heal people, and I'd like to learn. Do you think your teachers could teach me too?

"That's Menachem, the senior teacher." Ezra pointed to the tall Brother with the dignified bearing. "The one who makes the medicines is called Nissim, and this is Rachamim."

"How do you feel now, little lamb?" Rachamim asked.

"Wonderfully better," said Yedidyah, warming to this Brother with the kind dark eyes. He wiggled his foot in its wrapping of clean cloth. "The pain's almost gone!" Did you make Ruhama better too?"

Rachamim slipped a strong arm round Yedidyah, propping him up. "See for yourself. She looks better now, thanks to the Nameless One."

"Do you mean the Lord? Did He help?"

"All healing comes from Him, and Him alone."

Yedidyah knew better. For him, healing had come from the singing and the moving hands. He looked over at Ruhama, who was now sleeping peacefully, and her breathing was quieter. Even her hair looked more alive, her cheeks faintly flushed. "But all of you did something too. I watched you."

"We did what we did. But without His grace, nothing can happen."

Nissim brought several little packets of herbs. "Steep these in boiling water," he told an anxious Leah, "and let him drink. He must rest a few days, and all will be well."

"How can we thank you?" Leah asked.

"Yedidyah can think of ways. Be sure to do it when you are well, Yedidyah, and let Ruhama join you in whichever ritual you have thought of."

"He'll do it," Leah said, "for myself I brought these." She offered a basket.

"Give it to Menachem."

Menachem took the basket with respect. A nest of purple figs, covered by their own broad leaves, brought a smile to his calm face. He picked out a fruit. "For you, Mother," he said. Leah tried to protest, but he silenced her with a wave of the hand.

"And this is for the child." He offered a fig to Yedidyah, who accepted with pleasure. Ruhama's father was next, and a fruit placed near Ruhama. When Menachem had distributed all the fruit, he went over to Amnon with the last one. Amnon took it in disbelief. He'd done nothing to deserve this favour from the Brother, and this un-expected kindness brought fresh tears.

"Sometimes there is pain when healing starts to take place."

"I'm not sick."

Menachem's eyes were gentle. "Loneliness can hurt."

"I thought, if I could be near the little one…"

"It's not the little one you seek, Amnon."

"How did you know my name?"

"I asked," Menachem said simply.

"What do you care about the likes of me?"

"You came."

"So?"

"You came. That is enough. You'll come again." He placed a comforting hand on Amnon's shoulder, but Amnon shrugged it off, faintly alarmed. Nobody touched him. He wasn't sure if he wanted to be touched. How did this stranger know so much about him? He needed to get out of the house fast. Scrambling to his feet, he ducked out of the door.

Reuven gathered his brother in his arms. "Will I see you again?" Yedidyah asked Nissim. "I want you to teach me how to heal."

"First you need to be quite better yourself! "We'll be here tomor-row to check your foot; see how you are."

"I'll show you my sheep when you come. Did you put Sheleg in the pen, Reuven?" Reuven laughed. "The child loves the sheep more than us."

The Brothers crossed their arms over their chests, right over left, in a gesture of blessing, and started for home. Daylight had just broken.

Chapter Four

Tabernacles

The high holy days of the New Year and Yom Kippur, the Day of Atonement, were past. Throughout the country, each Jewish family had built a Succah, a small tabernacle, where they could eat and even sleep during the festive week of Thanksgiving. In ancient times, farmers had erected such temporary shelters as they gathered the harvest. Now families honoured the festival by living in similar booths, often vying with each other to decorate them.

"How I wish I could have gone to the Temple for the Thanksgiving," Sarah said, hanging a cluster of grapes from the wall of the booth her Joseph had built for the Feast.

"You'd never have been able to stand the crush in the Court of Women," her mother said, jerking her head at Sarah's grossly distended belly.

"Even so, perhaps I'll go tomorrow," Sarah said, "I'd hate to miss all the festivities."

"There'll be enough festivity here when the others arrive." Sarah's mother plumped down on the cushioned floor, fanning herself with a palm frond. "A first child at seventeen is a risky enough business without you rushing around in all this heat."

Sarah ignored her. "Our tabernacle is prettier than the neighbours', don't you think?" she said, admiring her husband's handiwork.

Joseph had built the walls of sturdy willow, which Sarah had hung with leaves and fruit. The tall palm branches forming the roof made a fretted ceiling for the sunlight to filter through and give light by day, and at night, the light of small oil lamps drew a dance of winged insects.

Sarah reached for a pear, sinking her teeth in the juicy flesh.

"The family is here," her mother said, ducking out of the leafy doorway to greet them. But it was only Joseph, his usually cheerful face drawn and worried.

"Joseph, you seem troubled. What's happened? Come and sit down, I'll send for wine."

"No Sarah, wait. There's something I have to tell you first." He carefully set down the precious articles he carried; a pointed palm branch, a gleaming citron, and the willow and myrtle branches which were waved in worship every day of the holiday.

She waited, uneasy, for Joseph to speak.

"There is bad news," he said.

"Joseph, what is it?" Sarah felt her face flushing, thinking of the hated Romans. What business had they to come to her country and interfere in its affairs? Couldn't they have stayed in their own country? "The soldiers have orders to let us worship in peace, haven't they?" she asked. "Did they again try to bring impure articles into the Temple? Isn't it enough that their idolatrous gold eagle's still there, right over the main gate?"

"Sarah, nobody desecrated the worship. It was beautiful. So many people, such rejoicing. There were wonderful offerings of fruits and grain, enough to feed the poor of Jerusalem the entire week of the Festival. The eagle's still in place though. No one dares take it down, as it's there by Herod's orders. Poor puppet of Rome, how he hopes to please. No, it's far worse than that. The worship was over, and I was starting for home when I heard the Romans have arrested four of our people, Zealots from Galilee."

"Why? What have they done?"

"It seems they were inciting the people to rebel against that coming census I told you about."

"You did, but I can't remember what it was for."

"It's for taxation. What else? You know how the Zealots feel about paying taxes to Rome. This isn't the first time they've refused to do so. Anyway, one of their leaders, a man from Galilee, came here to Jerusalem, and started stirring up trouble. He pointed out that this coming census represents the subjugation of Jews to Rome. Of course, we all know that, but this Zealot went one step further, and went around urging people not to co-operate in the counting. Naturally, the Romans were eager to stop him. They've had enough rebellions. So they arrested the man, together with three of his followers, and threw them all into the Antonia fortress."

"What will happen to them?"

"I fear the worst." Joseph sighed, shaking his head. "These same four have caused trouble before. The Romans could make an example of them."

Sarah's eyes widened. It was unthinkable. "Will they be put to death?"

"I'm praying it won't come to that."

Her baby lurched in her womb, and she placed a protective hand over her belly. "Poor young men. Is there nothing you can do to help?"

"I want to draw up a petition. Have it signed by as many members of the Sanhedrin as I can, and then present it to the Roman Procurator."

"But Joseph, you said yourself the Sanhedrin has little standing with the Romans. What help can come from a Court which tries Jews on matters of religion only?"

"I have to do something. I have to try. I'll ask Naftali to help me with the petition as his knowledge of the Roman tongue is excellent." He paused. "Sarah, about the family; they don't know anything of this sad affair, and I don't think we should tell them. Can we try to act as though nothing has happened, and let them at least celebrate one night of the Festival in peace?

"I'll try," she promised, getting up to greet the guests. Wearing bright festive clothes, her parents and unmarried sisters, her brother and his wife, pressed eagerly into the Booth. They exclaimed in pleasure over the decoration, admiring everything, settling good-humouredly on the cushions, moulding them to their contours, as they waited for the meal to be brought.

"The Temple's looking wonderful," Sarah's sister said. "So much has been done to it since we were last in Jerusalem. There must be thousands of workmen there. Herod will be remembered for his building," she chirped.

"And for his infamous cruelty," her husband muttered under his breath.

Joseph was relieved when the servant brought the meal, and the talk turned to food. The cook had flavoured the vegetables with herbs, their pungent aroma mingling with the delicate scent of rice gilded with saffron. There was curd sweetened with wild honey, and a heaped basket of fruit and nuts, a true harvest feast. The guests ate heartily, eyes shone, and laughter bubbled as the red wine worked its magic. Only Joseph and Sarah were sad, unable to force much gaiety, and Joseph got up before the meal ended.

"I have some business I must attend to," he explained, taking a fruit from the basket.

Sarah looked at him with raised eyebrows.

"For the donkey," Joseph explained, going out.

* * * * *

The Succah at Naftali's home was lavishly decorated. Silks from India glowed in purple and green, clusters of ripe grapes hanging heavy from their folds.

Solace

"Blessed be he who comes," Naftali greeted, welcoming Joseph in. Amos, Naftali's father, back from trading in Greece, broke off regaling his guests with stories of his journey to embrace Joseph warmly. Amos was extremely fond of his closest friend's sons, and especially of Joseph, who had spent much of his childhood in Naftali's company. As Amos talked, Joseph noticed Tamar. She's changed, he thought, his quick eyes taking in the swelling breasts under the faded rose of her garment. Compared to her mother Rachel, a dried-out prune in her red silk dress, Tamar was a ripe peach, ready for plucking. As she stood to welcome him, her wide skirts swayed, tiny bells tinkling on slender ankles. She smiled at Joseph, but her eyes sought Naftali's, her glance warm, sensual, passionate. Naftali's face betrayed nothing.

As soon as he could, Joseph detached himself from the others. "I want to speak to you alone," he told Naftali, "It's urgent."

* * * * *

When the Festival was over, Naftali returned to teach in the village. The petition had been signed and presented, and he and Joseph waited, impatient, for an answer. Days strung like beads on a drab necklace, hung heavy in the oppressive heat of a summer that had outstayed its welcome. The longed for rains had not yet fallen, tempers were frayed, Naftali's pupils drowsy and unresponsive.

Naftali tried in vain to arouse their interest, and distract his own mind from the forbidden image to which it clung. Often he had to bite his lip to stop himself saying her name aloud. 'Repeat after me, children, Tamar, Tamar.'

In the synagogue, trying to pray, Tamar's form rose unbidden before him; her long hair, her eyes, her breasts, filling his thoughts, stealing his attention from his unresponsive God. At night, fearing the sin of spilling his seed, Naftali was often forced from his bed to quench the sword of desire in cold water.

"I'm like a man possessed," he confessed to Joseph. "I think of her, nothing but her, day and night."

"And how does she feel about you?"

"When she looks at me, I sometimes think she feels the same way. Naturally we haven't spoken about it. We haven't even touched hands now that she's a grown woman."

"There's nothing I can say to help. I know what it's like, as you know. I sometimes feel so guilty when I look at Sarah, especially now she's to have a child. I tell myself I didn't choose to fall in love with

33

Pallas after my betrothal to Sarah. It was as if love chose me, and I was helpless to deny it."

"At least Pallas isn't your sister, Joseph. Tamar will be married in a year."

"I didn't know she was even betrothed."

"She will be soon. She's twelve already. Father came back early from Greece to start negotiations with the family of Manasseh, who have a son of marriageable age. Oh Joseph, can't you tell me there's still a way? You've studied the Law. Tell me there's still a way. In the days before Moses it was possible. The Egyptian Pharaohs were brother and sister. Tamar is my half-sister only. Why is modern law so firmly against it, Joseph?"

"You know the answer as well as I Naftali. You say Tamar is to be betrothed soon. What would happen if you and Tamar were to lie together? Do you want her to die? You remember Ruth, don't you?"

Naftali closed his eyes, trying to shut out the memory of that unspeakable day. The circle of grim-faced men with stones, the woman's screams, her futile attempts to protect the child in her womb. Ruth had died still clutching her abdomen.

Joseph sat silent, respecting Naftali's need for privacy. Then he said, "Leave home, Naftali. Come and stay with Sarah and me. I can't promise that not seeing Tamar will help, but at least it will keep you from temptation. You'll be safer with us."

"Yes, thank you Joseph, that's wise; but I'm afraid I won't be very good company."

"We're always glad of your company. Don't you know that by now? You are welcome in our house, to stay as long as you like."

* * * * *

Naftali took to walking the streets of the city after teaching the children, hoping to tire himself so much he'd be able to sleep. But the sights and sounds of the market place only reminded him of Tamar. He wandered past piles of bright pomegranates, heaps of grain, and their beauty was Tamar, her breasts, her secret places. Copper pots gleaming in lamp-light reflected Tamar. He watched women examining jewellery, bargaining with the vendors, and thought of Tamar. That I would buy for her, and that. I would thread those jewels in her hair, put rings on her fingers, wed her to me with gold. In the streets of the perfume sellers, he would turn as the scent of Egyptian kyphi, favoured by Tamar, caught his nostrils. The spice market assaulted his senses with pungent aromas hot and sensual as India, even the caged song birds reminded him of her.

Returning late one night to Joseph's house, Naftali was jolted roughly from his fantasy.

"The petition for the Zealots failed."

"What will happen?"

"They are to be crucified."

"Surely not. Not all of them. Is there nothing to be done?"

"Nothing. It's to take place tomorrow. All four of them to die. I can't go. I can't Naftali…can't face it. Sarah's distraught, and I'm going to stay here with her; but you can help. Go to Rachel and tell her to prepare a strong potion to dull pain…perhaps she knows of something more potent, something quicker. Ask. And tell her to have it ready for the execution tomorrow."

Chapter Five

Numa Ben

"Mother has prepared the potion," Tamar told Naftali, "but her head aches so badly, she can't leave her bed. Abishag, you'll have to come with us."

Tamar's little servant recoiled. "May I stay here, with Yael? I could tend the garden. I could bring cooling drinks to Mistress Rachel. She needs me here."

Tamar said sternly, "Abishag, I can't go out beyond the city walls unattended. You know that. Naftali will come with us, but I need you to help me with the cups. Keep your eyes down if you must, and you won't see much. Immediately I take the cup from you, you can go and stand farther off, with Naftali."

She handed a cup to Abishag, and took the other herself. Naftali carried a tall staff, forked at the end, which would enable Tamar to raise the cups to the lips of the dying. They walked in silence, Tamar leading, wide black skirts and heavy veil billowing behind her in the wind. Hot and dry, the Hamseen wind had been blowing from the desert for two days now, and Rachel was not alone in feeling its effects as it brought sickness and strange moods to the city.

Outside the walls, at the place of execution, a small crowd had gathered. A little apart from the rest, the women from Galilee, mothers and sisters of the condemned, huddled together in dumb despair. There was no sign of the prisoners as yet; but a group of rough Roman soldiers in short tunics bandied coarse pleasantries as they waited by four upright poles set deep in the stony ground.

Abishag hid her face in Tamar's skirts as guards dragged in four young men, roped together by their necks, naked bodies dripping sweat. Muscles bulging, the men pulled against the bloodied ropes, wild eyes staring through long tangled locks. A muffled groan rose from the spectators, but the prisoners kept silent, defiant. Only the youngest flinched as a soldier kicked away a starving dog, saliva drooling from its jaws.

Breaking from the hands of her sisters, a woman ran towards the prisoners, calling her husband by name. "Azariah, Azariah."

Surprised, the soldiers pulled swords, holding them across her path.

"Azariah!" She flung herself to the ground, hands scrabbling vainly in the dust as she tried to touch his feet in farewell. One of the soldiers yanked her up by her hair, sending her reeling back to the other women.

As the Hamseen wind died, a dreadful calm descended. Then the sickening thud of hammers as the soldiers drove in the nails, the shuddering gasp for breath as the crucified were hoisted aloft. Naftali felt his bowels heave, forcing a vile fluid to his mouth, while frustration and anger denied him tears. He handed the staff to Tamar, who fixed her cup firmly in its prongs. Alone and unflinching, she walked forward to the base of the first cross. Abishag, lips screwed tight in a white face, set off after her, carrying the second cup. Putting it down hurriedly, she ran back, head lowered, to Naftali's side as Tamar offered the cup. The crucified shook his head, but Tamar persisted, talking gently to the man, and after a while he consented and drank. Tamar continued her grim pilgrimage, until each prisoner had drunk from the cup. The guards didn't interfere; it was common practice for pious Jewish women to attempt to ease the torments of the dying.

As she returned from her mission, Tamar was met by three men in white. They stopped, and the older man stretched out his hand. Tamar passed him a cup, which he inspected briefly. "You did well, my daughter," he said, "they will not suffer long." He raised a hand to bless her, and the three walked towards the crosses. Heedless of the purity of their garments, oblivious to the stench of faeces already swarming with flies, the Brothers prayed with the condemned.

One of the onlookers started a hymn. His voice, tremulous at first, rose in a passionate plea to the Shekinah, the Angel of Mercy, to take Her sons swiftly. As others took up the plea, the Angel spread protecting wings of cloud, dark with promise of rain, which obscured the sun, and softened the sight of the last contortions of the dying.

Standing in the growing dusk, a young rabbi addressed the doleful crowd. "Brothers and sisters, women of Galilee, the pain of our men will soon be over. Even now they are on their way to the footstool of the Most High. I tell you that they won't die in vain! Others will arise to strike a blow for freedom, and freedom will be ours! The sacred ground of our holy land will once again be free for the Children of Israel to worship and live as they want. Nothing is ever lost in the struggle for justice." The crowd stood hushed. It was the sixth hour; darkness was falling, and people straggled home.

Only the Galilean women stayed. One of the mothers, crazed by grief, shuffled to the foot of the cross where her son hung dying. Sitting on the ground at his feet, rocking her body like a cradle, she croaked an ancient Hebrew lullaby, the familiar words floating on still air. "Numa ben, numa ben. Sleep my child, sleep my son."

Chapter Six

The Stunted Sheep

Shafts of wintry light beamed from the setting sun, rimming the clouds with radiance.

It will be a cold winter, thought Boaz, intent on bringing his flock home. Narrowing his eyes in the luminous dusk, he looked out over the hills. Outlined against the sky, three small figures skipped one behind the other. Yedidyah danced ahead, playing a flute, elfish locks flying. Next came Ruhama, a slight child dressed in blue, clapping her hands to the tune, while fat little Shoshana panted gamely after her. Sheleg brought up the rear, trotting happily behind. Seeing Boaz, Shoshana waved a plump hand in greeting.

Boaz, wrapped in thought, lead his flock home.

"Miriam," he said, warming his hands around a steaming bowl of broth, "I'm afraid that Avinoam and Leah will go hungry again this winter. They'll never kill that sheep of Yedidyah's for food, that's for sure; the boy's so fond of it."

"It will be a lean hard winter for them," she agreed, "and Leah is with child again. But I've heard that Avinoam is making a new type of lamp. If it sells, they'll be able to buy more grain."

"There's not much to be had, Miriam. I've been thinking how we could help them."

"Will you give them provisions? We haven't got so much ourselves."

"That stunted sheep of mine, the one with the brown spot on the back. It can't be sold for sacrifice. Have we enough wool for clothes this year?"

"More than enough. Were you thinking of giving them the sheep for food?"

"I'll give it in exchange for new lamps for the Festival of Lights. That way they'll be able to accept it, and won't feel indebted.

Miriam thought of the row of lamps, simple pottery dishes with a lip at one side, which she used for the Festival of Lights each year. Set in the windows of every home at night, the tiny flames braved the darkness, patterning the whole village with their cheer. She would place the new set of lamps round the room, making a warm glow of festive light. "It would be good to give the sheep," she said.

* * * * *

39

"I'll call him Ketem" Yedidyah said, looking lovingly at the stunted little sheep with the brown marking.

Boaz smiled, but Leah cut in sharply, "Oh, no, my son, you will not call him by name. You have your own sheep, and that is enough. You won't even take this one to pasture. Reuven can take him."

Avinoam came in with the lamps in his hands. "I have another lamp for you," he said. "Yedidyah, bring the new lamp for Boaz."

With Yedidyah out of the room, Leah explained, "We'll take the sheep quickly to be slaughtered, before the child has a chance to get to love it."

Yedidyah came back with a small red lamp, which he handed to Boaz. The shepherd turned it in large capable hands, admiring the shape. This was a different kind of lamp indeed. Instead of a large opening at the top for oil, this one had only a small aperture, with a larger than usual spout for the wick. A handle at the side meant the lamp could be safely carried, with very little risk of the oil escaping. "How did you make this?" he asked.

"I press clay inside into a mould, and when I open it, there's the lamp. I make the handle separately, fix it in place, and set the lamp to dry in the usual way. Like this I can make many lamps quite quickly. I thought I could sell them in Jerusalem as well as in the villages. They can be carried by travellers, as they hold enough oil for several hours. Yedidyah made the handle on that one. He's done it well, it's neat and firmly placed. What do you think?"

"Yedidyah will be a good potter when he's grown."

"No, I'll be a shepherd like you, and have a flock, and each sheep will be given a name. I'll use them for wool only, and the ewes can give milk. None will go to the Temple.

Boaz ruffled the boy's yellow hair. "Here's a boy that knows exactly what he wants! Miriam will be happy with the lamps, and this new one will be useful to carry at night," he said as he took his leave.

"You promised to tell the story of the Festival of Lights, Father," Shoshana reminded.

Avinoam sat on the floor to tell the story, Shoshana on his lap, Yedidyah at his feet. "Do you remember I told you about the wicked king Antiochus?"

"Antiochus desecrated the Temple," his son interrupted. Yedidyah hated the Temple, a bloody place where so many lambs and birds had to die. "He brought a swine in there," he finished gleefully.

"What's swine, father?" Shoshana wanted to know.

"It's an unclean animal."

"Have you seen one?"

Avinoam spat. "No. I hope I never will."

"Tell about Judas Maccabeus, Father."

"I'm trying to. Judas went around the country rousing our people to fight the Greeks, who were here at that time with their heathen ways, and get them out of the Temple. The Greeks had trained soldiers, and much better weapons, but still Judas and his brothers fought them, and managed to force their way into the Temple. Then they threw out all the defiled vessels."

"What's defiled?" Shoshana asked.

"Impure."

"And then Judas put pure lamps in there, like these?"

"Yes. He put pure lamps there, but there was not enough oil to keep them burning. The flame in the Temple must never go out, but the Greeks were outside, stopping people getting in to bring more oil. And then Judas prayed to the Lord, and a great miracle happened."

"I know, I know!" Shoshana squealed, "The one lamp lasted for eight days. But how? Ours can't last more than a few hours, can it?"

"I expect Judas was a friend of the Lord," Yedidyah said. "Like me," he added under his breath, thinking of his uneasy truce with his father's God.

"Judas Maccabeus was a hero, and that's how he'll always be remembered. The miracle lasted eight days, and that's why we light lamps every night for eight days." Avinoam finished.

He sighed. First the Greeks, now the Romans. How he wished for a new Judas to arise and overthrow the might of Rome. That would need another great miracle, he reflected, thinking of the sad fate of the Zealot rebels.

* * * * *

"Shoshana, we're going to do the ritual today," Yedidyah said.

"We did it yesterday, and the day before that."

"Not properly, Shoshana. That was only practice. Today we're going to do it properly. I hope you remember how? It's got to be special—our very own ritual; not something everyone else does. That's why Nissim said we had to invent it ourselves.

"I know that Yedidyah. I was there when you and Ruhama first thought up the ritual. I helped, and you said I was useful. I'm five, not a baby any more."

"Go and get Ruhama," he ordered.

She ran off obediently, clutching her 'baby', a doll carved of wood, that Avinoam had brought back from Jerusalem for her. He'd wanted a present for his daughter to honour the Festival of Lights, and the wooden doll had not left Shoshana's side since. Not many Jewish children had a doll; they were images, forbidden by Moses, but Avinoam had decided that Moses had not been speaking of children's toys when he gave the Commandments. How could he? They probably didn't have dolls in those days!

The three children set off, Yedidyah carrying a large piece of coarse cloth. It had not rained for two months since the initial downpour after the Succoth festival, and there was still plenty of dry kindling to be had. Brittle stalks snapped off easily in the children's practised hands. They gathered a good-sized bundle, stuffed it into the cloth, and dragged it to their chosen spot.

"We'll make the fire now," Yedidyah said, "then there's something I need to tell you."

"We'll do the ritual first," Ruhama said.

"Yes, yes, of course." Yedidyah took a small piece of iron and a flint from his girdle, and worked quickly and deftly. Sparks flew, dried thorns and twigs caught fire, and soon there was a crackling blaze. The children sat around the fire in the growing dusk. Overhead, migrating birds wheeled to their resting places, and the moon rose, a brilliant crescent in a violet sky.

Yedidyah picked up his flute and played a simple tune, while Ruhama pulled a pomegranate from a fold of her skirts. Sharp nails bit into the resistant skin as she wrenched the fruit apart. She handed one half to Shoshana, and the two set to work. Soon a pile of translucent seeds, ruby red, glinted in the firelight on a flat stone.

"We're ready," Ruhama said.

Yedidyah stopped playing. "Shoshana, you go first."

Shoshana scrambled to her feet, holding her doll. She circled the fire three times, a solemn child, long skirts brushing the ground. She stopped, and began: "I say." The children clapped their hands twice in unison.

"I say." Again they clapped,

"I say, thank You for my brothers,'" she finished triumphantly.

It was now Ruhama's turn. As she circled the fire, Ruhama's face, framed by untidy braids, glowed with satisfaction. "I say," she began, and they clapped as before.

"I say, I say, thank You for my healing."

Yedidyah marched purposefully round. "I say, thank You for my walking," he offered. "Now stand up, hold hands, repeat after me. We the children,"

"We the children,"

"Help each other,"

"Help each other,"

"And help all animals,"

"And help all animals,"

"As long as we live,"

"As long as we live,"

"Amen."

"Amen."

They sat to share the pomegranate. Sparks from the fire rose in faery bursts, spangling the darkness. Firelight burnished Shoshana's long curls as she bent over her 'baby,' holding it tenderly to her breast.

Yedidyah's pale locks were a halo for his head as he exclaimed, "I have to save the sheep."

Two pairs of eyes looked at him expectantly.

"It must not die," he went on.

Ruhama reminded, "The sheep was given to your family for food for the winter."

"I won't eat it!" Shoshana burst out.

"Nobody will eat it; I'll save it somehow."

"The slaughterer is due to come in a few days, and take it and others to be killed for food. There's nothing you can do."

"I'll think of something. Haven't we just promised to help all animals? I'll take it away somewhere."

"You can't take it away," Ruhama was practical. "Where would you go? Besides, it's not yours. Taking is the same as stealing, isn't it? You can't steal food from your own family."

"They can buy grain. Nathan has enough to sell, I heard father say so. We always ate grain before, and nobody starved."

"Your mother has a child in her belly."

"It can't eat yet."

"I've heard say a woman has to eat well if the child is to be born healthy."

"Then I'll get money and give it to Father to buy more grain so we can all eat well."

"I have a coin I can give," Shoshana smiled.

"I have two," Ruhama added. "How many do you have, Yedidyah?"

"Only one, like Shoshana. Aunt Rivka gave us one coin each at Passover."

Ruhama scratched marks in the ground with a stick. "Four coins." She shook her head. "Not enough, Yedidyah."

"I'll ask Aunt Rivka for more. I'm sure she'll give them to me. She was sorry about Hamoud. I know she'll want to help save the new sheep; I know it."

"Your Aunt Rivka lives in Bet-Lehem, doesn't she? It's a long walk. At least three hours. How will you get there? You don't even know the way."

"I do know it. I went to Bet-Lehem at Passover, with Reuven. I walked all the way back, as Aunt Rivka was on the donkey. I didn't even get tired. I can go and ask for the money, and come back and give it to Father; then he won't kill the sheep."

"Father will never let you go," Shoshana shook her head knowingly.

"I won't tell him. I'll wait till everyone's asleep, then I'll go."

Frightened, Shoshana cried, "You can't go in the dark. How will you see? You might fall again. Wolves may be there." Her voice tailed off in a sob.

"Don't cry, Shoshana; look at this!" Yedidyah felt in his pouch and produced a lamp. "I can light my way with this. It's the new sort, and won't go out when its carried."

"No," Ruhama insisted, "Yedidyah, don't go alone. Please, we'll think of something else. Don't do it! Don't go!"

"Don't do it Yedidyah," Shoshana echoed.

Yedidyah sat quietly, thinking. "I know someone who will come with me," he said at last. "He'll come if I ask him. He saved me when I hurt my foot, and yesterday, when I took Sheleg to graze, he was waiting for me. He said he cared for me. He'll help."

"Mother will cry," said Shoshana.

"I'll be back by mid-day. She need not know I've gone. Shoshana, you must tell her I went out very early to take Sheleg to graze. If I'm not back in time, you'll have to tell her the truth. I went to visit Aunt Rivka, but not alone. Someone went with me. That way she won't worry."

Chapter Seven

Abomination

The night air was cold and crisp, the stars exceptionally bright, so Yedidyah and Amnon had no difficulty following the winding track leading to Bet-Lehem. Yedidyah carried his lamp, and Amnon a strong staff.

"What will your mother think, Yedidyah, when she wakes in the morning and sees you're not there?"

"She'll think I've gone out early with Sheleg. That's why I took him with us. He walks well, don't you think? But we need to be back by mid-day tomorrow."

They continued their walk in silence, hurrying along the stony track, panting with exertion.

"We'll rest a little, here," said Amnon, pointing to a rocky hollow at the edge of the track.

"We should not rest," said Yedidyah. I must get to Bet-Lehem quickly, and then when I have the money, start for home. I have no time for resting."

"But I am tired. I'll make a fire, and we'll lie down to rest. A short while only. After that, we'll have more strength, and we'll be able to finish our journey more quickly."

"Not yet, not yet," Yedidyah panted, pressing on, though he was getting very tired. It had been a long day, and the night was nearly over.

Towards dawn, as the first houses of Bet-Lehem appeared in the growing light, Amnon said, "We'll rest now, and visit your Aunt by daylight. She'll be frightened if we knock at the door while she's still asleep."

Yedidyah was reluctant to agree, but they were nearly there, and a short rest would be most welcome. Amnon lit a small fire in a spot sheltered from the track by two boulders, spread his cloak on the ground, and lay down. "Come, lie down besides me," he coaxed, "and sleep for a short while."

"A short while only," Yedidyah said, faint with tiredness, as he lay down next to Amnon.

* * * * *

An unusual sensation was coming from his groin. Yedidyah, half asleep, found it not unpleasant. Heavy with drowsiness, he tried to focus on the feeling. What was it? With a start, he realised that someone was caressing him. He felt a vague alarm pierce the pleasurable sensation. Naftali had warned the boys about abomination. Could this be what he meant? He'd better get up quickly, before something worse happened. He tried to pull away, then realised he was being held in a firm grip. Frightened, he struggled to free himself, but his childish strength was no match for a grown man. "Eli, Eli, help, save me," he panted, but Eli couldn't have heard, because then it was happening. The hard insistent pressure on his backside turned into a driving red-hot agony. He thought he would die, the pain was so bad. He lay still for a moment, while Amnon murmured endearments, stroking his hair. So this was abomination. A forbidden sin. And it had happened to him! Outraged, he fumbled for a stone. Somehow, he twisted his body round, and with all the strength he could muster brought the stone crashing down on Amnon's temple. Amnon groaned; his grip slackened. Yedidyah, maddened and terrified, hit him again and yet again, till blood splattered the rocks, and Amnon lay quite still.

Chapter Eight

Two Miracles

It was the month of Kislev; days of bright wintry sunshine cooled by freshening winds, nights of cold starry skies. On the Eve of the Festival of Lights, Jerusalem, high on her hills, wore a light dusting of snow, as Tamar and Abishag walked quickly through the streets. Tamar glowed in a red cloak, while Abishag, in nut-brown, squirreled a covered basket to her child's chest.

Arriving at Sarah's house, they burst rosy-cheeked into her room, shedding their cloaks in a heap on the floor. Tamar warmed her hands at the brazier of coals, inhaling the fragrance of pine with which it was sprinkled.

"Sarah, Father bought rose-water and almond paste for the festival, and we made sweets for you. Look, how beautiful they are. Take them, we'll have a feast." She kissed her friend's flushed cheek. "How are you, Sarah? And Joseph, is he well?"

"He's tired, Tamar. Since he's been elected to the Sanhedrin I don't see him so much. But he's happy enough. Now that he's got a vote, we hope he'll be able to make the others see things his way, perhaps soften the law a little. It's too harsh as it stands. Can I keep the sweets for tomorrow?" She pressed a sweet into Abishag's willing mouth. "Actually I haven't been able to eat at all today."

"Too full of child," Tamar laughed. "Father bought me a shawl. Look how delicate it is. He says it's made from the beard of a goat. Imagine! The overseer had to bring it back from India, as Father's too busy arranging my betrothal to go anywhere himself."

"Do you know anything about your betrothed? Who will it be Tamar? You don't even seem very pleased. I was already married at your age, and look at you, almost thirteen, and not even betrothed." Sarah eyed Tamar's slim waist, girdled with a red silk cord. "Don't you long to be married?"

"I know it's my duty to marry and have children. How else will Father have grandchildren? Naftali refuses to marry, he says he has no taste for it. To be honest, I too feel much the same way."

"What about babies? You'll want them once you're married. Especially if you marry a man as kind and good as Joseph." Sarah slumped back on the couch, shutting her eyes.

"Don't you feel well, Sarah? I keep chattering about my own affairs, I forgot to ask you how you are feeling."

"I'm so big and swollen today, I can hardly move. Can't even eat. I hope the child will be born soon; I'm longing to hold him in my arms, get him out of this huge belly." She smoothed down her voluminous robe, and Tamar looked thoughtfully at her bulk. She'd seen many pregnant women, she'd helped at many a birth, but never had she seen such a gross distension. Sarah's pretty round face, framed in glossy black hair, seemed not to belong on this monstrous frame. "I see the carpenter brought the cradle." She gestured to the corner, where a cradle hung suspended on forked wooden supports. "It's beautiful. Can we look?"

"Of course."

The girls admired the smoothness of the cradle, sniffing in the scent of the new wood. Abishag rocked it wistfully. A child of uncertain parentage, she had no chance of marriage and babies. "It won't be long now before you rock him to sleep in it," she said enviously.

"Just one cradle, Sarah?" Tamar asked.

"What do you mean?"

"I've thought of something. Sarah, let me listen to your baby." Sarah looked puzzled. "Lie down. Trust me. There's something I want to check." Sarah lay down obediently on the couch, and Tamar knelt beside her, pressing her ear to the distended belly. She stayed there several minutes, hair mantling Sarah's robe, eyes closed in concentration.

"Well, Tamar?" Sarah asked as Tamar lifted her head. "Did he talk to you? Will he come soon to his longing mother?"

"There are two children in there, Sarah. I heard two heartbeats. You are to have twins!"

Sarah's eyes lit in astonished delight. "A double blessing! Are you sure? We won't tell Joseph yet. Let it be a double surprise for him when it happens." She gasped, pressing a hand to her belly.

"Have you a pain? Is it starting?"

"I've had pains all day. I thought it was nothing but indigestion from the rich food we ate yesterday. Now I feel it much stronger." She clutched at Tamar's arm. "Could it be that the time has come? I'm afraid, Tamar. What shall we do?"

"Don't be afraid, we'll help you. Abishag, go quickly and tell Master Joseph to send for the midwife."

"What if I die,? I'm going to die. I don't want to. Aaiee, the pain! It's there again. It hurts so much. Help me, stay here, don't go away."

48

"I won't go," Tamar soothed, taking Sarah's hand, "In a little while you'll have your babies; it'll all be over soon." Sarah clung to her, whimpering, as Joseph came in. Crossing to his wife's side, he looked at her with concern. "I've sent for the midwife. She'll be here soon. Is it bad, my love?"

Sarah was writhing now, sweat bursting out on her forehead. "Go away, Joseph, it's women's business," she panted.

* * * * *

"I'm going mad with worry, Naftali," Joseph said, as they crouched outside the door. "How long can it take? She's been there since yesterday afternoon, and already day is breaking. What if she dies? Isn't there anything we can do? Can't we try again to get Rachel to come?"

"Tamar is just as skilled as her mother in these things. "Sarah's in good hands. Just think how many children that old midwife must have brought into the world."

"Perhaps she's too old, and can't be of much help."

Sarah's cries were becoming hoarse and feeble; and still no sound of a new-born cry. Still crouched on the ground, Joseph began to pray.

"The child is in the wrong position," the midwife said wearily, "See, the bottom is presenting." She reached for a knife.

"Do you want to kill her?" Tamar hissed, pushing away the woman's hand "We can turn it. Help me." She started to massage, grunting and pushing, while little Abishag tended to the failing mother, mopping the dank brow, feeding her drops of a herbal infusion to relax the tense muscles.

Milky sunlight was already trickling in through the high window when at last Sarah screamed, and a tiny body slithered out into the midwife's hands.

"A boy, a beautiful boy," Tamar exulted. The child, perfectly formed and plump, though a little bruised, cried out at its expulsion to a vast world, and Sarah's eyelids fluttered open, seeking her son. The tired midwife held him up for her inspection, then turned to care for him.

"Now the other," said Tamar.

"No other, no other." The old woman busied herself with the infant.

"There was another heartbeat," Tamar insisted.

"I couldn't hear another."

"Let me listen again." She bent her head. "It *is* there, I can hear it. Still there, but faint."

The midwife ignored her. She washed the baby, rubbing the tiny body with salt before wrapping the infant securely in swaddling clothes. She held up the child, only its diminutive face visible under the bands. "Show Joseph," Sarah whispered.

"Sarah, see, the baby is laughing," Abishag said, as the child opened its bud of a mouth.

Sarah, too tired to smile, gasped as a fresh wave of pain engulfed her, and a second, smaller child, burst like a seed from a pod into Tamar's hands. But this one wasn't crying. Tamar laid the still form on its mother's thighs. Taking a hollow reed from the midwife's bag, she placed it in the minute nostril, sucking sharply, but the baby lay inert. Desperate, Tamar pursed her lips, blowing her own life into the child, her mouth over his face, willing him to live. As the air inflated his lungs, the child drew quivering breath, and a thin wail rewarded her efforts. Triumphantly raising the little one, whose scrap of manhood proclaimed another boy, she cried, "Sarah, Mother, look at your second son."

Sarah, speechless with exhaustion, only glanced briefly at the child. To her, the room with its lone beam of dusty sunlight was a peaceful heaven, and Tamar an angel in a soiled robe. Now she could sleep.

By the time the astonished midwife returned to the bedside, followed by Joseph, treasuring his son in his arms, all was in order. Abishag had sprinkled herbs on the coals to freshen the air, filling the room with fragrance. Joseph halted at the foot of the bed, amazement giving way to delight at the sight of a second boy, lying swaddled on the coverlet besides his mother.

"How do you feel, my love?"

Sarah tried to raise a tired hand in greeting, but let it fall. "She must rest," said Tamar, congratulating Joseph on the double blessing. She scooped up the baby from the bed, and handed him to Joseph. Joseph, standing proud with his twin sons, said, "Thank you, Sarah."

"What are the names?" Abishag asked. Joseph smiled. "The first is Mattiah, gift of the Lord."

"And the second?"

Tonight will be the second night of the Festival of Lights. There'll be two lamps lit in honour of the miracle. This child is our second Miracle, so that will be his name. He is Nissim, Miracle." He raised his hands to bless his wife "Greetings, Mother of Mattiah and Nissim. Sleep peacefully, rest and be strong, the nurse is already here to take care of you and the babies." He motioned her forward, a thick-set woman with dark skin. "Her name is Devorah." But Sarah was already asleep, Tamar and Abishag curled up together on a heap of cushions, at her feet. Joseph left quietly.

Chapter Nine

The Nut Garden

It was evening when Tamar awoke, and two festive lamps already glowed at the window. Sarah was still asleep, and the nurse dozing by the fire. Abishag, scrubbed and fresh in a borrowed yellow dress, was sitting by the cradle, ready to call the nurse should the babies wake and cry.

"Stay here and help Sarah this week, Abishag," Tamar said impulsively, going in search of a servant to bring her fresh clothes and help her bathe. She would ask Naftali to bring her home.

Clouds, low in the night sky, parted fitfully to reveal the moon, then drew together to hide it, jealous of so much beauty. Tamar and Naftali walked home together quietly, each deep in thought. When they were nearly there, Tamar said, "Naftali, there is something I need to say to you." Naftali waited. "I'm to be betrothed soon, and married within the year; but my heart will not be wholly with my husband." Naftali ached to touch her hand, but kept his own muffled in his thick cloak.

"My heart has only one love," Tamar said softly, "His name is Naftali."

Naftali listened, incredulous, as Tamar went on, her words, like heavy drops of honey, stirring the depths of his cup of longing, raising bitter-sweet ripples of desire.

"I've loved you ever since I first saw you. I can't count the days I've longed for you, breathed for you, bathed my body for you. My heart beats to the rhythm of your name, Naftali, Naftali."

Naftali's words surfaced slowly, from somewhere deep inside. "I, too, breathe your name. Even through my prayers. Tamar, you've become my whole Temple of worship. Your courage and your skill, your laughter and your beauty, all these I have made into a prayer shawl, and wrapped it round my body. But you're my father's child, and the Law says we may never be joined."

"So must we sacrifice our love on the altar of the Law?"

He couldn't answer. They entered the silent house, and he went straight to the mikvah, hoping to numb the terrible intensity of his emotions. Stepping into the cold waters, he screwed up his eyes to drown out her image, tried to pray.

The long awaited rains began to fall even before he left the mikvah. Not troubling to dress, Naftali wrapped himself in his cloak, and went barefoot to the garden to welcome the life-giving downpour. As the thirsty earth offered herself up to the rain, the fragrance that rose from their union filled the air with a sharp clay perfume. Rain-drops washed leaves and flowers, and streamed down his uplifted face to enter his parted lips. He went further into the garden, stopping to stroke the tender buds of the almond tree, rubbing his hands over the glistening bark of the walnut.

Then he saw Tamar. She was standing motionless in the rain, her back to him, bowed head uncovered, long hair unbound. Naftali halted, and she turned. For a long moment the two stood unmoving, then each took a step towards the other. Naftali opened his arms, and Tamar nestled into them. Her head reached just to his heart, and she laid it there, pressing her cheek to his chest. He folded her to himself bending his head, kissing her damp hair which smelled of honey. They didn't speak, but stood swaying together struggling with longing. Finally, she took his hand, and lead him further into the garden, pushing through tangled vegetation to find a hiding place.

"Wait." He plucked blossoms from a bush of fragrant white flowers, pushing them into her hair. Smiling, Tamar slipped a hand beneath his cloak. Naftali moaned, and drew her to the ground, "Rose of Sharon, precious dove." He covered her generous mouth with his own.

"I have longed for this night, my brother, my love," she whispered. Trembling, Naftali parted her upper garment, baring the small breasts. "My sister, my bride." He lifted her heavy skirts. Then feeling the resistance of her virginity, he tried to draw back; his sister must come a virgin to her betrothed. But Tamar was eager to receive him. Eagerly thrusting her body upwards, she offered herself to him like the earth to the sower of seed.

Unwilling to part, oblivious to the rain, they clung together, breathing endearments. "Tamar, you are crying," he explored her face with his fingers.

"I am fulfilled, and filled so full I can't contain it."

"Bride of my heart, Field of Wheat," he soothed, cradling her, stroking away the tears.

"You, too, are crying Naftali."

"I've experienced perfection, Tamar, and already weep for its loss."

"So we can't come together again?"

"Tamar my love, you know it can't be."

"What will we do?"

"I'll go away before your betrothal, and not come back till you are safely married."

"She twisted her fingers in his hair, pressing her warm mouth on his. "This is what I'll remember when my betrothed lies with me. Will you too, think of me?

"Every day. I'll go on breathing your name, 'Tamar, Tamar.' Be assured you are wound round my heart, and I'll love no other."

"Prove it to me one more time."

She clung him like a creeper round a tree, breathing endearments, as all his pent-up days of restraint burst freely from his body.

Hours passed, and the first bird song was heard in the rain-washed garden.

"Come, my sister, we must go into the house before it's light. Go now Tamar, I will follow later."

She pushed through the wet undergrowth, crushed blossoms still clinging to her hair.

Chapter Ten

Menachem

Amnon could hear them approaching. As they came nearer, he tried to focus his eyes. Three men dressed in white, and a youth, were walking in single file, leading a laden donkey. He knew them! Those were the Brothers who had healed the boy, the child who had trusted him...until that thing had happened. Amnon shut his eyes against the painful memory. His head hurt so much it was hard to move and he turned his face towards the boulder in shame, hoping he wouldn't be recognised. But the men stopped. Someone laid a gentle hand on his shoulder, and the calm voice he remembered so well, was asking what had happened. Amnon kept quiet.

"There is blood on his temple."

"Let me see."

He could hear liquid being poured, feel a dampness as a cloth was pressed to his head. He flinched as a throb of pain knifed its way inside his head, then sat, eyes shut, allowing them to tend him.

"Drink."

The potion was bitter, clearing his head, shocking him into a reality he preferred not to face. He closed his lips against more.

"Drink some more, it will help you." Still he pursed his lips, and the cup was taken away.

"He will have to be tended."

"It will take time. Shall we take him with us?"

"I know this man," Menachem said. "He's from Bet-Zayit, near Jerusalem. We'll have to help him back there, if we can lift him onto the donkey."

Amnon remained silent behind the closed eyes. He could hear more travellers approaching, talking loudly...something about the Temple, and doves for sacrifice.

"Be quick, Ezra, we're blocking the way. Help me get him on the donkey." Menachem said. "Unload the gifts, you'll have to carry them with you; but leave a little food and water with me. I'll take him to his home, where I can tend him."

"Couldn't we come with you?"

"No. Continue on to Bet-Lehem, and I'll try to join you there by nightfall."

Strong arms round his body, lifting him, the crunch of sandals on stones as the travellers passed, "Go in peace, go in peace."

The jolting of the donkey, the arm still supporting him as he slumped on the little beast. He would have fallen had he not been held. Where was Yedidyah? No. He didn't want to think about that. Blot it out, swallow it down into the swirling fog in his head. Forget. Try to forget. How long they walked he didn't know. There was sun on his shoulders, but he shivered in the warmth. "Thirsty," he groaned.

Menachem's arm, strong and steady, and the water, cool on parched lips. He drank, averting his face from the winter sun.

"We're nearly there," Menachem encouraged, as the donkey stumbled over the stony path.

"What happened?" a woman asked. "Did he get robbed? It's Amnon, isn't it?"

"He's been hurt. Can you tell me which is his house?"

"That's the house, over there by the terraces, and his father is working in that field."

"Please go and tell him I have brought his son."

Then he was home; Menachem helping him down, guiding him firmly inside. Resist, Amnon thought, resist, there is something I must resist. Shivering, he collapsed on the sleeping mat which made up his bed. His father came in, full of concern, and covered him with a blanket. "Tell me what happened. How did he get hurt?"

"It's a deep head wound, which I've already cleaned," Menachem said, "but as you see, it was on the temple, and it certainly stunned him."

"Where did you find him? Did he say how it happened?"

Hide, hide, thought Amnon. Best not to know how it happened.

"We found him on the road to Bet-Lehem. I don't know how it happened, he's no state to talk, and must be kept quiet. If he rests, and drinks this potion, he'll probably be able to talk in a few hours."

"He was gone all night," the worried father admitted. "Ruth tells me Yedidyah, son of the potter, is also missing. His father was out looking for him this morning."

'Yedidyah.' The sound of that name struck forcibly at Amnon's defences, gained a painful entry, made him groan aloud.

Menachem's quiet voice betrayed nothing. "If you stay with your son, I'll go to the boy's family and inquire."

"Will you come back?"

"I'm on my way to Bet-Lehem and need to be there before nightfall, but I'll come back to check Amnon briefly and then I'll tell you what I know."

"Won't you sit and take some refreshment, you must be tired."

"Thank you, I should go now."

"Is there nothing I can do for you?"

"The donkey is tired. He's worked hard. If I leave him with you till I return, would you feed and water him? I'd be grateful." Menachem raised his hand in blessing, and left.

* * * * *

Leah was alone in the house, spinning wool, the long thick strand taking shape under her skilled fingers. She jumped up when Menachem came in, and he could see the worry on the thin face, under the smile of greeting.

"Blessed be he who comes. I'll bring water. Please sit down." She indicated the one thin pile of mats, the family's only furniture. Leah called Shoshana, who came running, her cheeks pink under the tumbling curls. Seeing Menachem, she hung back, suddenly shy, but he motioned her near, admiring her doll, patting her hair, thawing her reserve.

"Will you get your father, Shoshana?"

When she had gone, Leah burst out, "We don't know what to do with Yedidyah. He ran off to my sister Rivka in Bet-Lehem. All that way at night. He could have been attacked by wolves, or lost the way, or fallen again. Whatever can we do with a child who doesn't obey us? He's got more respect for you than for his parents. Do you know he performed that thanking ritual you asked him to do, practised it for days, and made Shoshana do it too. If you talk to him, he might listen. Rivka will bring him tomorrow."

"Please try not to worry, Mother. I think I may be able to help. You see..." He stopped as Shoshana erupted sobbing into the room.

"Yedidyah wanted to save the sheep. Now it's too late." She turned on Avinoam who had followed her inside. "You're cruel. I'll not eat it, ever!" She flung herself to the floor in the corner.

Avinoam ignored her. "You heard about Yedidyah? Not only does he defy his father, but now Shoshana is copying his ways. What is a father to do? Where is the respect for a parent? I'm going to give him such a beating when he returns, he won't disobey his father ever again."

"I understand someone is bringing him back from Bet-Lehem tomorrow. But tell me, did he go there alone?"

"All I know is he went all the way to Bet-Lehem at night. Of course no-one went with him. What madman would encourage a son to defy his father?"

"Shoshana?" Menachem asked gently.

"What?" she sniffled.

"Do you know if anyone went with Yedidyah?"

She shook her head. "He said he would ask someone to go with him," she mumbled into her hands.

As Menachem digested this unwelcome information, Leah pulled her daughter onto her lap, rocking her like a baby. "We wanted Yedidyah to learn to read and write, but now there is no teacher. Naftali sent word he's going away, and won't return to teach in the village. Who else will we find, to come all the way from Jerusalem? Yedidyah loved that teacher. Now he'll have even more time to think up mischief."

"He'll have more time to help me in the pottery," Avinoam said half-heartedly.

"Avinoam, how many pots can you make? Already there are rows of pots waiting to be sold," Leah reminded.

"The new lamps sold well."

"Now everyone is making that sort of lamp. How many can we sell?"

"I think I know how I can help you," Menachem said slowly. "Would you let Yedidyah come and study in our school? He could learn to read and write, both in Hebrew and Aramaic, to count and to pray, and later a trade, according to his aptitude."

Avinoam was already nodding in approval, when Leah interrupted. "But you live so far away, how could he come home?"

"He'd stay in Qumran. Some of our married members live just outside the settlement, and care for the pupils."

"No!" Leah clutched Avinoam's sleeve. "He's our son, and I'll not give him to others to care for."

"He'll always be your son," Menachem reassured. "We'll bring him to visit. It's not so far. A scant two day's journey on foot, even for a child.

"We haven't any money to pay for his keep," Avinoam said.

"There would be no need. We adopt the boys we teach, and care for them as our own."

"And where would he live?" Leah wanted to know. "Is there a proper house for him? You told us Qumran was destroyed by earthquake many years ago. Where would he sleep? On the bare ground?"

Much as Menachem wanted to be on his way to Bet-Lehem, he wrestled with the need to take time to convince Yedidyah's parents. Yedidyah was needed at Qumran. With no children of their own, the celibate Brothers relied on their adopted pupils to swell the ranks of the elect community, and trained them carefully in the Essene tradition. Without pupils, the community could die out.

It was nearly nightfall. Time to leave. He could come back and speak to these people another day. But just as he got up to go, several villagers came in.

"Brother Menachem comes from the shores of the Sea of Salt," Avinoam said. "He's going to tell us all about the community there. Maybe Yedidyah can go and study there."

Menachem didn't want to waste too much time talking about the Settlement, but most of the villagers had never seen the sea in their lives, and interrupted constantly as he talked. "Nothing grows near the Sea of Salt," said practical Boaz, "Some even call it the Sea of Death. And I've heard the rainfall is less than in Judaea; so how can you water crops?"

"When it rains, waters come crashing down the cliffs, and we trap them in conduits which lead to large cisterns. There's enough water to drink and bathe in, and enough to tend small crops."

"No one can live on small crops. What about grains? What about vegetables? Here we have olives we can sell and use the money to buy grains; there you have nothing," said Boaz.

"There are two oases nearby, to the south," Menachem said, trying for patience, "and date palms grow in abundance. Those dates are the sweetest in the land. We also grow vegetables there and enough barley for bread. No one goes hungry in Qumran. You should come to visit, and see for yourself," he told the doubting shepherd.

Ruhama, who had crept in, and was sitting as near Menachem as she could, put in bravely, "Yedidyah will never eat meat."

"There's no meat eaten in Qumran." We raise enough grain, fruit, and vegetables to feed our people and our guests. We've a bakery as well as a kitchen, and there's a special room for washing clothes as well."

He should never have mentioned the laundry room. Now there were excited questions about such a rare commodity. Seeing the villagers so impressed prompted Avinoam to ask, "What do you say Leah? Shall we send our boy to study with the Brothers?"

Leah shook her head. "This is his family, and we can't let him go. He's our child, he was born here, and here he belongs. I'd miss him too much. Of what use is a son when he's far away? First, let him come safely back home; there'll be plenty of time later to talk about school."

"Leah! We'll discuss this together alone," Avinoam said sternly.

Ruhama asked, "Mother of Yedidyah, when is Yedidyah coming back? I thought he would have returned with Amnon."

"What's this about Amnon? Is it possible Amnon went with him?"

"They set out together, but Amnon is already back. I heard it from Ruth. It was Brother Menachem who brought him. Hasn't he told you?"

"Why wasn't I told? What right had Amnon to take my son and then come back without him? If he's hurt Yedidyah, I'll kill him," Avinoam said, balling his fists threateningly.

"Why should Amnon harm Yedidyah?" Ruhama was puzzled. "He promised to help him. He said loved him."

"I'm going to see for myself."

Menachem, remembering a child's sandal on the path near the place they had found Amnon, laid a restraining hand on Avinoam's shoulder. "Amnon is sick."

"Tell me how you found him. Did he mention Yedidyah? Was Yedidyah with him? Tell me."

"We found Amnon with a wound on his temple, alone on the road to Bet-Lehem. He was dazed, and could hardly speak, so I didn't question him. I merely brought him to his home."

"Someone must have attacked them both, and Yedidyah ran away," Avinoam guessed.

Leah screamed.

"Calm yourself Mother," Menachem soothed, "We don't know what happened until we question both of them."

Boaz said grimly, "Maybe Yedidyah hit Amnon."

"He'd never do a thing like that," Leah protested.

"It could be he was defending himself," Boaz explained.

Leah clawed her garment.

Avinoam yelled, "If he's hurt my child, I'll drive him from the village; I'll beat him so hard he won't live to see another day." He rushed for the door, the villagers after him, but Menachem barred the way.

"Let me get at him!"

"We don't know if he did harm the boy. It won't help you to beat him. You say Yedidyah's returning tomorrow? First talk to him, and hear what he has to say, and I'll go now to Amnon, and question him."

"I'm coming with you."

"Better that I go alone. He may not talk at all if he sees you are there. I'll be back tomorrow and will tell you what I know. Before that you can speak to Yedidyah, and find out what happened. Will you wait?"

"I can't promise. I must find out what happened to my boy."

What shall I do if I find Amnon's harmed the boy, Menachem asked himself, as he hurried off. If I leave him to Avinoam, he may kill him, and have to face the Sanhedrin, and the penalty for murder. But if I help Amnon escape, I'll be sinning by aiding an evil-doer, and myself have to pay the penalty.

* * * * *

Amnon's fever blazed. He burned under the woollen blanket as demon thoughts prodded and poked at him.

Menachem laid a cool hand on his forehead, holding a cup to his lips. "Drink."

He drank obediently. "Tell me what happened with Yedidyah"

"I didn't mean to harm him." His hand went to his male member, flaccid under his robe. "I should wrench you off, lustful thing. If it was not for your greed, I would not have forfeited the trust of the child."

He waited for Menachem to berate him, but Menachem was silent, forcing himself to stay calm.

"Why don't you condemn me?"

"You have condemned yourself. I have no need to condemn."

"I know that you love that boy. Why aren't you angry?"

"Should I be angry? Tell me what happened."

"I only wanted to caress him. I swear it. But this one-eyed fool tore itself out of my hand, pushing at the child."

Menachem swallowed disgust. "Go on."

"He hit me. That's all I know."

Amnon's father wailed, "What did you do? Amnon, son, what did you do? When Yedidyah comes back and tells his father, Avinoam will beat you, and drive you from the village. He could kill you."

Menachem steered the frantic father away from the bed. "Come, we'll think what to do."

Noach tugged miserably at his scanty beard. "I've always tried to be a good father to him. His mother died when he was born. I should have remarried for the boy's sake. That it should come to this. We are disgraced. What shall I do?"

"Have you any family outside the village?"

"Only one brother in Jericho."

"Take Amnon there. Leave immediately."

"He's much to weak to walk. As soon as Avinoam finds out what happened, he'll come and beat him. He'll kill him."

"I'll leave the donkey with you. Take Amnon to Jericho on it. But Amnon must return it to us at Qumran as soon as he is able."

"Why are you helping him?"

Menachem reflected. It was a question he was to hear again. Why should a member of the Brotherhood at Qumran, a Son of Light, help an evil-doer? He looked at Noach pensively. "I can't say. Perhaps it has to do with the dawn tonight of the Star of Forgiveness."

Chapter Eleven

Immanuel

Loud and clear, the local rooster shrilled the new day. Faint fingers of light creeping cold through the narrow window, pried open Rivka's puffy eyelids, and she shivered awake. She must get up, there was so much to do. First, she admitted reluctantly, she needed to wash, then there was bread to bake for tomorrow's journey, extra water to draw, the hens to be fed.

She sighed, lumbered to her feet, reached for her shawl. The old door was stiff on its leather hinges, and she pushed it hard. It groaned open, and Rivka stepped outside. Picking her way through the littered courtyard, she squatted over the privy. Meagre drops of scalding urine trickled thinly, and Rivka shook her head, peering disconsolate at her swollen feet. Surely there must be some herb to ease this discomfort? Perhaps in Jerusalem she'd find a skilled woman to help.

The water pan was nearly empty. She hesitated, then dipping a hand briefly in icy water, brushed hasty fingers over her face, and dried it on a corner of her shawl. Enough of washing! Now to fetch water.

Back in the house, she picked up the largest pitcher, and started for the well, moving slowly on bloated legs, bracing herself against a freshening breeze. Rounding the wall enclosing the few houses, she halted in disbelief.

Pale and filthy, Yedidyah crouched against the stones, his sheep at his side. At the sight of his aunt, he scrambled to his feet, staring at her mutely, waiting for her reaction.

Rivka loosed a torrent of questions. Whatever was Yedidyah doing in Bet-Lehem? What had happened to make him come? Was he alone? She hustled him inside, the sheep at his heels. "Does your mother know you're here?"

He shook his head, trembling with cold, too distressed to answer.

Rivka fetched a blanket, and wrapped it round him. She tried to take him in her arms and stroke his hair, but Yedidyah resisted, pulling away.

"Are you hungry?" She crouched over the fire-pit, fanning the flame. "I'll make bread. The neighbour has a little goat's milk. Would you like that?"

Shrunk inside the worn blanket, the child picked at the edges, unravelling a strand, balling it up in nervous fingers. One sandal was missing, his feet bruised and blue.

Rivka soothed, "You're safe now child. Won't you tell me what happened, so I can help you?"

He seemed to be searching for words, mouth pursed, blue eyes blinking, but she could see he wasn't ready to talk yet. She'd make the bread. She measured barley flour into the large pottery bowl, added water, kneaded and pounded. Stripping crisp dried leaves from the stalks of herbs hanging from the rafters, she scattered them over the dough, working them in with the ease of long practice.

When she'd set the bread near the fire to rise, Yedidyah still hadn't spoken. Rivka picked up the pitcher. "There's no more water, so I'm going to get some. I'll bring milk too. Stay here, keep warm, I'll not be long. Stay here," she warned. Yedidyah appeared to have understood, for he nodded. and drew back, turtle-like, into the shell of the blanket as his aunt hurried out.

At the well, she didn't stop to gossip with the other women, but drew water quickly, walking home as fast as her stiffened joints allowed. Leaving the jar outside her house, she went to the neighbour, returning with a small pitcher of milk, warm from the goat.

Even before she opened the door, she heard impatient grunts coming from inside. She flung open the door to find Yedidyah standing in the kitchen alcove, holding the knife. Rivka stared in dismay. Yedidyah, grunting through clenched teeth, grabbing at his hair by the fistful, was sawing it off, flinging it to the floor. His furious face defied her to stop him, and she was forced to watched helplessly, not daring to interfere. Finally he dropped the knife, and passed a hand over his despoiled head. Tufts stood out absurdly here and there.

He looked so comical, Rivka felt forbidden laughter welling up inside her. She tried to control the urge, but it was too much for her. Her nephew glared in astonishment, as Rivka started laughing. Powerless to stop, she went on laughing helplessly until her legs weakened, and she collapsed on the bed, holding out her arms.

A faint smile dawned on Yedidyah's lips. Then he was in her arms, and she was rocking him, wiping the tears that started in earnest down the grubby cheeks.

"It was because of my hair," he sobbed. "I hate my hair. He said I had pretty hair." He shuddered. "He stroked it."

"Who stroked your hair, Yedidyah? What are you saying?"

"I think I killed him."

"No, no," she consoled. "How could you kill anyone? You're still a child. Tell me everything that happened, from the start."

"He put his…" He couldn't continue.

"His what, lamb?" Rivka asked, suddenly grim.

"His…" Yedidyah grimaced in disgust. "Naftali said it was abomination. So I hit him with a stone. He bled so much I think I killed him. I think he died! So I ran away. I came here."

Rivka's anger blazed. *Whoever it is, I'll kill him myself, if the boy hasn't already done so. Surely this appalling thing couldn't have happened to her innocent nephew, not to Yedidyah, not to this child?* Her eyes went to the knife on the floor. *If I find the man who dared touch this boy, I'll cut off his manhood. He won't touch a child again.*

She had to know. "What did he do? Did he hurt you?"

"I can't speak about it." He struggled to his feet, and she saw there was a streak of blood on the back of his thigh. "Mother will be worried. I have to go home."

Rivka forced a smile. "First you need to tell me why you came. Was it to see me?"

"Oh, I had forgotten." He spilled out a garbled tale about wanting to save a sheep intended for food, and his need for money to buy grain for the family, so they wouldn't feel deprived.

"I wish I had money to give you, love," Rivka said, gesturing round the poor room with its sparse furnishings. "Even if I did give you coins, there's not much grain to buy this year. When there's not enough rain, the harvest is small. I think you know that." She made herself go on quietly, for the sake of the child, though seething inside at the unspeakable awfulness of what had happened to him. "Your Sheleg is a fine animal; try to content yourself with him. That new sheep you were given is needed to feed the family, and its fat can be used for fuel."

She bent to put the small clay oven over the fire-pit, and a tear trickled onto the risen dough as she searched for words. "Do you know what I think? I think that when a sheep is eaten, its body goes on living in the bodies of people who eat it."

He looked at her, incredulous, while she floundered on, "I feel it doesn't die, because it nourishes people, and that's how it helps us. Can you understand? There is a prayer to thank the animal we eat, and thank the Lord for giving it to us. Do you want to stop it doing something useful?

"It doesn't have to die to be useful. It can help by giving us wool. I wanted to save it, but it's too late now."

Rivka had no answer to this. Instead she said, "Your family will be worried. I'll send a message with villagers going to Jerusalem today. As for you, you must stay here and rest until tomorrow, and when I go to Jerusalem for the census, you can come with me."

* * * * *

It was night when he awoke; stars already glittering in the sky. He ate hungrily, stuffing bread into his mouth, not bothering to say the blessing.

"Have you lost your manners along with your hair?"

"I forgot." He looked at his sheep with concern. "Sheleg is hungry, he needs to graze, and I'll have to take him to the fields. I'm not tired, so may I stay with the shepherds tonight?"

She knew the shepherds well; they were good lads. It could help, being in their company. "Go if you must, but don't stay out all night. I'll leave the door ajar for you, and you should come back to sleep before we go tomorrow. It's a long walk." She handed him his lost sandal.

"Where did you find it?"

"I went to the trail leading to Bet-Zayit. I knew you would have come that way."

"Was anyone there?" he asked fearfully.

"No one."

"He didn't die then."

"No, he didn't die."

He looked relieved. She watched him as he ducked out of the door. He was limping slightly, and her heart was bitter.

* * * * *

At the Inn, preparations for the evening meal were finished. A rich lentil stew, spicy and inviting, bubbled in the blackened pot. Platters of bread and olives, decorated with sprigs of herb, stood ready on long low tables. The Innkeeper busied himself with the wine, while the serving girl piled raisin cakes, sweet, warm, and stuffed with pine nuts, onto plaited reed mats.

Yerusha, the Innkeeper's wife, was tired. So many guests, the Inn so full, and still they came; the young, the old, some with babes in arms, sucklings too young to be left at home. Yerusha would be glad when the census was over and she could rest. Periodically she'd stop and put her hand over her belly, which swelled slightly under the rough woollen robe. A look of fierce concentration crossing her pleasant face, she'd feel for movement, a sign of life; but the babe lay unmoving. Then she would shake her head sadly, thinking of that other one, born so still, and buried so swiftly in the stony ground.

There was a knock at the door, but the landlord didn't bother opening it, as the Inn had no room for more guests. Let whoever it was find somewhere else to spend the night.

Another knock. "The Inn is full!" he yelled, didn't you hear what I said the first time?" He wrenched the door open. A bearded man stood there, holding the halter of a grey donkey which carried a cloaked woman.

"My wife needs help. She's near her time."

"I've already told you this Inn is full," he said roughly, "Didn't you understand? What sort of a husband wanders abroad with a wife about to give birth?"

"We wouldn't take up too much space. I'll stay outside."

The landlord shook his head, but as they moved away, something about the man's quiet dignity moved Yerusha, and she plucked at her husband's sleeve. "The barn," she said.

"What about it?"

"They could stay in the barn tonight, as it's so cold outside. Tomorrow they can leave. May they stay in the barn?"

He assented grudgingly, and turned again to the wine vats.

"Ruth, see to the tables," Yerusha ordered. Tonight she wouldn't help serve dinner in the inn; she had guests of her own. She sucked in her breath, delighted with her plan. Back in the kitchen, she took bowls off the shelf, filled them with sweet curds, and put them in a basket together with two fine loaves, a handful of raisin cakes, and a jar of olive-oil. On an impulse, she crossed to the carved wooden chest, took out a small bundle, placed it carefully on top of the basket, and hurried out.

She hardly needed her lamp. Every stone on the path stood out clearly, outlined in light. A necklace of stars, so low she could have plucked it with her hand, garlanded the humble barn. At the entrance, Yerusha set down her lamp as its tiny flame seemed useless; the moon was strangely bright tonight.

The young woman had loosened her veil, revealing dark hair framing a face of youthful purity. Why, she's scarcely more than a child, Yerusha thought.

The girl started to speak, and Yerusha moved nearer to hear. As she listened, she forgot her own secret pain. It was as if she was being drawn down into the gaze of this stranger, whose dark eyes revealed a well of boundless compassion, though her words were simple. "I think the baby's coming," she said, feeling for Yerusha's hand. "It's sooner than we expected. We would never have left home if we'd known, but we needed to go to Jerusalem for the census. I thought we'd be safely back in Galilee in time for the birth, so I brought nothing with me for the baby. All our baby clothes are at home, and of course the cradle too. My husband made that cradle himself, it's really beautiful. Now I have nothing. No bed for the child, and no clothes either. What shall I do?"

"Have no fear, he can sleep in the straw, it's fairly clean as the animals are out, and see, I brought clothes." Yerusha opened the bundle she'd placed in the basket, her hands trembling slightly as she took out clean swaddling bands. These were the garments her first little son had never worn, and she hadn't looked at them since; afraid lest the child she was now carrying might be still-born too, and have no need of them.

The young mother almost forgot her pains as she held up each small garment in turn, even managing a smile as she admired the careful stitches.

"Did you make them? They're beautiful! Fit for a prince. How can I thank you?"

"Would you pray for my child?" Yerusha pointed to her swollen belly.

"The clothes are for your own baby. When will it be born?"

"In the month of Sivan. But it's not moving. Already the fifth moon, and still it doesn't move."

Again the look of infinite compassion. "What's your name?"

"Yerusha bat Matityahu."

"I am Mariam, my husband is Joseph," she said, her voice strangely comforting, "I'll pray for your baby, Yerusha bat Matityahu."

"May the Lord hear your prayer. When my baby is born, if it lives, I'll call it Mariam."

"Even if it's a son?"

Yerusha smiled. "First let me help you."

Yerusha had helped at many a birth, though never in a stable. What a blessing this young woman was young and strong. She did the best she could to comfort and ease the mother, and after a short labour, Mariam was delivered of a healthy son.

Yerusha used the olive oil she'd brought to clean the baby, and wrapped him in the bands. Laying the child in his mother's arms, she took the clean napkin from the basket of provisions, and spread it over the hay at her side. "Now he has a bed."

The new-born opened eyes the colour of the sky in summer. "A prince of Israel," Yerusha admired. "What will you call him?"

"He is Immanuel."

"Immanuel," echoed Yerusha, "Immanuel, God with us," she cried, laughing with joy as the child in her own womb leaped into vibrant life.

* * * * *

The shepherds had lit a fire in their brazier, and sat warming their hands, talking and laughing. Yedidyah didn't feel much like laughing, but he felt safe here, and decided to stay until Sheleg had eaten his fill; though it might take a long time, with grazing as poor as this.

He jumped up when someone laid a gentle hand on his shoulder.

"Shalom, Yedidyah ben Avinoam."

It was Nissim. Nissim who had helped heal Ruhama, and who had healed him too, when he'd hurt his foot. He wound his arms round the beloved Brother, burying his shorn head in the consoling warmth of the white robe. "Nissim."

"Will you come with me, Yedidyah?" Nissim asked quietly.

"Where are we going? And what about my sheep?"

"Trust me, Yedidyah, come with me, and we'll take the sheep as well."

Yedidyah asked no further questions, but let himself be lead to a nearby barn. Menachem was there, standing outside, and with him were Rachamim, and the boy Ezra. Who could have known they'd be here? In spite of his pain, he felt a pleasant sense of anticipation. Whatever was happening, he was glad to be a part of it.

It was hard to see anything in the barn at first, there was so much light. Then he saw her; a girl with such a sweet face, lying in the hay, with a baby near her. The Brothers were standing with arms crossed in blessing, and some of the shepherds had crowded in too. Yedidyah hid behind them. He mustn't come too close; he was unclean; a boy who had done bad things. But he felt a pressing need to see the baby, so he dropped to his knees and shuffled forward in the hay, craning his neck until he could see the infant quite clearly. If only he could touch him, just once. He knew he shouldn't, but he caught the mother's eye, and looked at her inquiringly. She was looking at him with understanding, as if she knew what had happened to him. It didn't seem to matter to her that he had been defiled; this lovely mother didn't care.

She was smiling at him, and beckoning him close to her, and it was a most marvellous thing that was happening, being allowed to touch the baby. Yedidyah stretched out a hand, and being very careful, stroked the soft down of the infant's head. It was all he wanted.

The Brothers came offering gifts, which they placed near the baby. Yedidyah knew it had to be a very special baby, because he could see the Shekinah, the Angel of the Lord, standing in the entrance to the barn. He'd never seen an angel before, but thought it must be her, as she fitted the description told him by his mother; very tall and shining. The Brothers didn't seem to have seen her, because they kept their backs to her, though the song of praise they were chanting was turning the whole barn into a place of peace and blessing. Yedidyah wanted to stay for ever in the warmth and love, but all too soon the Brothers were leaving, and motioning him to go with them.

Walking home through the fields with Nissim, under clouds, like lifted wings, Yedidyah asked, "Brother Nissim, how did you know that baby would be born tonight?"

"Our astrologers saw it in the stars. They told us this night a special baby would be born. So we came to bring gifts."

"Did the astrologer tell anything about this special baby?"

"They said that he is to be King over all Israel."

"Is that all? Only a King? I think he's more than that!"

"What could be higher than a King?"

"The Shekinah said he would be Yeshua, the one who saves."

"A king to save his people?"

Yedidyah didn't answer. Eli had deserted him on the road to Bet-Lehem, but a new friend had come to take his place, a friend sent by the Lord Himself, so the Shekinah had sung. As the image of Eli faded, Yedidyah slipped his hand into that of Immanuel, and found it fitted perfectly. "Yes," he whispered, I'll walk with You."

Chapter Twelve

Weep Bet-Lehem

Joseph and Sarah's house was a hive of activity as preparations got under way for the feast to be held on the day of the twin's circumcision. A bright bee in his striped robe, Joseph bumbled happily through the house, attending to all the details needed for the comfort and delight of his guests. He was sparing no cost. Merchants came and went, bringing fruit from the warmer climate of Jericho, fresh vegetables from the fertile north. Hunters brought succulent pheasants which would be plucked and roasted, while servants combed the market for the rarest herbs to flavour the birds. The house filled with the mouth-watering scent of fresh bread and spicy honey cakes, plumping and browning in the ovens.

Sarah stayed in her quarters, resting and suckling her babies. Still weak from the birth, she found it an effort even to greet her own sisters, who had already arrived with their husbands from Hebron. Sarah's mother guarded her daughter jealously, making sure no man came near the room. Even Joseph had to content himself with speaking to her from the foot of the bed. A woman who had born a child was unclean until she had undergone purification in a special ceremony, and Joseph would have to wait many weeks before he could even touch her hand. But he came every day to admire the babies, who slept in identical cradles, watched over by the devoted nurse.

In all the bustle of preparation, Naftali was able to slip away unnoticed. There was a small courtyard leading off his room, and here he withdrew, needing to be alone. The courtyard was surrounded by a high wall from whose old stones tiny yellow flowers sprouted. The gardener had worked well; bright butterflies fluttered round cyclamen and narcissus, birds feasted on berries or flew twittering from tall broom bushes to the solitary tree.

Sitting in the wintry sunshine, his back to the gnarled tree-trunk, Naftali relived his union with Tamar in his mind. Anxious not to forget a single precious moment, he wove them into a careful web, stringing its flimsy structure with memories. Rousing himself to pray at the prescribed times, he found with astonishment that his prayer, formerly so lifeless and dull, was now filled with fervour and devotion. It seemed to him he was unable to distinguish his love for Tamar from his love for God, and in his confusion, he passed the soft warm hours of the afternoon worshipping his goddess together with his God. Not wanting to join the noisy throng of family and friends for meals, he lived on dates still soft from the palm, and curds as innocent as the breath of the babies.

Joseph's words slithered lizard-like into the flimsy fabric of his thoughts, breaking the web, jerking him into a harsh reality. "Will you be Godfather to one of the twins at the circumcision?"

When Naftali didn't reply, Joseph went on "I know it seems strange I waited so long to ask you, but I've given it careful thought. Out of all the family and friends, it's you I want. All the family will be here, and it's going to be a wonderful feast. Later, I thought you could come with me to the Temple on the thirty-first day for the Redemption of the First Born. Don't look so startled, Naftali. You surely didn't think I was going to give up my sons to the service of the Temple? We'll offer redemption money, even if it does cost me a double sum." He beamed happily, thinking of his plump babies. "Naftali, are you listening? You appear to be in a dream."

"Joseph, I don't know what to say."

"Say 'yes, I'd love to be godfather to Mattiah.' Say 'I'd love to join you in the celebration, and I'll come to the Temple too, for the Redemption ceremony.'"

Naftali was suddenly acutely aware of the criss-cross pattern made by his sandal on his bare foot. "I'm honoured you asked me, Joseph. I would love to be godfather to Mattiah. How I would love it," he added wistfully.

"That's settled then, you'll be one of the godfathers."

"No, Joseph, I can't."

"Don't be absurd, Naftali. Why ever not? I'm not going to let you refuse."

"There are others more worthy than I."

"What do I care about being worthy or unworthy? You're my dearest friend. That's what counts. I'm asking *you*, not anyone else. You get the greatest honour as Mattiah is the first-born. Sarah's brother has already agreed to take second place, and be godfather to Nissim."

"Joseph, I can't take part at all in the ceremony. I certainly can't go to the Temple on the thirty-first day." Naftali kept his eyes lowered, inspecting the dust.

"Naftali, what's happened? I don't understand. Can you explain?"

Naftali spoke into the dust at his feet. "I need to purify myself."

Joseph was visibly relieved. "Is that all? Well do it! Use the mikvah here. Or if my mikvah isn't good enough for you, go to the new bath outside the Temple, and purify yourself there. What further purification could you possibly need?"

Naftali said miserably, "I haven't asked the priests, but I think I need at least at least eighty days."

"Naftali, you can't be serious? Please tell me this is all a mistake?"

"No mistake."

"Is this the friend whose biggest pain was caused by a longing to feel the Presence of God in prayer? Whatever could make you feel contaminated, pure soul?"

"I don't feel contaminated, though the Law would have it that I am. I've loved her so long, Joseph. It seemed so pure, so perfect, when we consummated our love."

"Tamar!"

"Yes, Tamar, my sister Tamar."

Joseph sighed audibly. It must have been the night the twins were born, he thought. Tamar left with Naftali, and I didn't try to stop them."

"You say nothing Joseph. Are you shocked?"

"No, I'm not shocked, just sad. For both of you. I'm sorry it had to be this way, but you didn't plan to fall in love with Tamar any more than I planned to love Pallas. Like yours, my love didn't go away because the Law says it was forbidden, so I do understand a little of how you must feel. No, I'm not shocked, I'm sad. But shall we go inside and talk there, out of this rain?"

Naftali let himself be guided to a couch, and the two sat side by side. Faint sounds of laughter filtered into the room, birds still called as they nested for the night. Joseph covered his friend's hand with his own, listening while Naftali talked. Naftali started slowly, but once the stone of delusion was removed from the dam of his emotions, they flooded out in a torrent of words. He was impotent with rage at the idea of Tamar going to another's bed, sickened by the thought of the deception she must practise on her wedding night. All the beauty that should have been his alone, used and dirtied by some stranger.

"I've got to go away, Joseph, I can't bear to see her with another. She's lost to me. I've lost her, and I've lost my father too. How can I ever face him again, knowing what I've done? I have to leave."

"Have you thought where to go?"

73

"Greece maybe. I know I must decide quickly, but I can't seem to do it. All I really want is to see her again, to be with her, where I belong. I should share her life, I should father her children, it should be me, not some other who can never love her as I do."

"I think I may be able to help you."

"You should be looking after the guests."

"And aren't you a guest? Come on, we'll go to the bath-house."

Naftali stared.

"There won't be a bath-house like mine in the Sinai desert," Joseph said with a wry smile. Where in the Sinai desert is there a bath-house with heated water, and a fine mosaic floor?"

"What are you talking about?"

"I'll tell you on the way to bathe. First we bathe, then we eat. No, don't look so reluctant. I've noticed you haven't been coming to meals. You won't get such good food in the desert, and not in Egypt either."

"Egypt?"

"Tomorrow a caravan leaves for there. Join it, and do some purchasing for me in Alexandria. There are some hangings needed for the Temple. I would have gone myself, but of course I can't leave for several weeks. If you go, you'll be doing me a great service. It will mean my overseer can stay here, and help with the celebration, where he's needed. Would you do this for me?"

"Could I stay in Egypt, and send the carpets back with the caravan leader? I'll need to be away a longer time.

"Hangings, Naftali, not carpets. Yes, if you find him trustworthy, send the hangings back with the leader. But if something goes wrong with the transaction, expect to stay in exile for ever!"

Naftali didn't appear to have heard. He went obediently to the bath-house with Joseph, going through the motions of bathing in a trance-like state, toying listlessly with the food at table.

Later, sitting in the central courtyard after dinner, talking quietly so as to avoid disturbing the sleeping household, he said, "Joseph, there's something I haven't understood."

"It's really quite straightforward," Joseph said, "You have the money, and you know my requirements. Is it the measurements? Shall I explain again?"

"I wasn't thinking about Egypt, Joseph. I understand what I have buy there; have no fear. I was thinking about love."

"What is there to understand?"

"How is it possible that my feelings of devotion for God returned when I prayed this morning? Just when I thought I'd never feel that love again. As soon as I broke the Law, it came back."

"It was always there. You just lost touch with it. There is no separation in love."

"How could breaking the Law bring the love back?"

"I'll break a few more laws myself, and let you know!" He glanced at his friend's puzzled face. "Forgive me, Naftali, it wasn't meant unkindly; but it's late, and I'm tired. Whoever could be knocking at the door at this hour?"

It was Joseph's cousin Shelomo. He staggered in out of the rain, long hair and beard glistening wetly in the lamplight. As Joseph greeted him, Shelomo removed a sodden cloak, pungent with the odour of damp wool. Balling reddened hands into fists, "May his name be erased," he spat.

"Whose name?"

"Herod!"

Quick anger blazed in Joseph. "What has he done now, that spineless spawn of a dull mother?"

"I came as quickly as I could, but it's a long way from Jericho. Too long. I wanted to warn them, but it's too late." He shook his wet head helplessly, scattering driblets on the smooth marble floor. "I was there Joseph; dancing attendance at the summer palace; waiting for instructions for the purchase of building materials for the Temple...I was there, and I overheard..." Shelomo struggled with tears. Joseph, sick with apprehension, lead him to the couch, waiting for him to go on.

"I overheard the soothsayer."

Naftali brought wine, but Shelomo brushed it away. "The soothsayer told Herod the child had been born in Bet-Lehem of Judaea."

"What child?"

"The child Herod had been searching for. Ever since he heard the prophecy that a child would be born to be a greater king than he, Herod has searched for that child to kill him."

"And then?"

"Then Herod yelled 'call my guards', and when they came he gave orders."

Finally his horrified listeners heard the terrible news. Herod in his madness had ordered the slaughter of all the male children under the age of two in the town of Bet-Lehem.

"*My* babies," Joseph made to run from the room.

"No, no, Joseph," Shelomo said hurriedly," the babies of Bet-Lehem, not Jerusalem."

"My babies, Shelomo. Since the twins were born, and I'm a father, I feel a father's grief. Those babies of Bet-Lehem…unbearable…soldiers pulling children from their mothers. Oh monstrous." He clutched at his stomach, pulling at his garment as if to rend it.

Naftali asked, "Shelomo, can we still warn them? Were you on your way to do that? Perhaps if we all act quickly we can help at least some to escape?"

"The soldiers had better mounts than I. I came as fast as I could, but my old donkey is no match for horses."

"My horse is strong and fast. I'll go," Naftali said. "Perhaps there's still some way to help. Perhaps they are not all…" He looked inquiringly at Joseph.

"Yes yes Naftali, you go and I'll come with you. Shelomo must stay here, he's travelled enough tonight."

Naftali opened the door and looked outside. Rain was pouring down as if in sorrow, wind howling a lament. "We'll have to wait till dawn. We won't be able to find the track in the dark, the rain will put out the lamp."

"There's an Inn outside Bet-Lehem," Shelomo said. "Go there, and speak to the Innkeeper. He knows all the families in the town. Ask him. Perhaps there is still something you can do."

Sending his exhausted cousin to his bed, Joseph sat down with Naftali to form a plan. At first dawn, Naftali and Joseph would ride to Bet-Lehem, each leading a strong pack-horse. First, they'd go to the Inn, and inquire there. If there were any fugitives to be found, they would bring them on the horses to Jerusalem, where they could join a caravan for Egypt.

Even before the first light showed through the rain, four horses stood snorting uneasily at the gateway, and Naftali and Joseph, heavily cloaked against the rain, set off for Bet-Lehem.

Chapter Thirteen

Penance

The four walked silently homeward down the winding path. Tall Menachem strode ahead, long hair lifting slightly in the wind, face calm and unruffled. Behind him, Nissim, short, stocky and brown-skinned, plodded stolidly under the weight of the water-skins, while Rachamim and Ezra brought up the rear.

Rachamim carrying a heavy bundle of provisions, as well as his spare clothes, eyed the road which wound implacably lower and lower, shimmering in the heat. Menachem doesn't seem to regret lending the donkey, he thought, glancing at Ezra, who had started to limp.

A vast sleeping animal, the many breasted desert glowed pink, red, brown and gold under a hazy sky. Nissim's voice, though low, carried clearly in the still air.

"Shall we go first to Jericho?"

Menachem halted, waiting for the others to catch up. All four set down their bundles, and stood, their shadows purpling the path, waiting patiently while Menachem reflected. "We're already late," he said. " Ezra is tired. We'll go straight home."

Nissim adjusted the band of cloth round his mop of tangled curls. Like Menachem, he was already a full member of the Council of the Pure, and so felt it timely to speak.

"Go ahead with Ezra, and I'll go to Jericho and fetch the donkey," he offered.

"You would not be home till after dark. We all go together to Qumran," Menachem decided.

There was nothing Rachamim could say. What right had he to offer an opinion? Even if he did survive the coming year of difficult tests and initiations and was accepted as a full member, he'd still have to defer to his seniors. That was the Rule. Trained not to show negative emotions, he hid his feelings, but anxious questions filled his mind as they walked on towards Qumran. The donkey was the property of the Community, so why had Menachem given it away to an evil-doer who might never return it? The donkey's loss had brought hardship to them all, as it had been used to carry their spare clothing and the provisions they always took when travelling. The freshly-filled water-skins were heavy, and slowed them down. Now they would not reach home at the appointed time. All this is going to be reviewed in Council, he thought fearfully.

He was still occupied with gloomy forebodings as they neared the small dwellings scattered outside their Settlement. Here the married members of the community lived, and a weary Ezra was delivered to his foster-parents. The exchange of greetings was brief. They were late and must hurry.

Rachamim's mood lifted at the first glimpse of Qumran. Nestling in the shadow of huge sculptured cliffs, the stone buildings drowsed golden in the setting sun. To the east, the waters of the Sea of Salt stretched smooth as silk, reflecting blue mountains edged with castles of pale blue cloud.

As the Brothers passed through the gates and stepped into the assembly room, Rachamim breathed in the familiar blessed stillness of home.

Twenty white-clad Brothers stood in a semi-circle to greet them, arms crossed over their breasts in the traditional salute. How good it was to see again the beloved faces, to immerse himself in the quiet discipline of the community. How cool the waters of the mikvah on his dusty body, how fresh the smell of clean clothes from the communal store.

At Qumran, hymns of praise went on all night, the Brothers chanting and sleeping by rote. After a simple meal of vegetables eaten in silence, Rachamim forgot his tiredness as he took his place in the white-clad assembly, singing the glories of the Nameless One. When at last, calmed by the prayers, he lay down to sleep in the company of his peers, Rachamim was at peace. Was not everything ordained by the Lord?. His former misgivings were mistaken, it was needless to entertain them.

Early the following morning he sat to meditate, facing east ready to greet the sun when it rose. Meditation that day was on the Angel of Joy. Concentrating on the centre of energy at the base of the spine, Rachamim invoked the Angel. His devotion and strength of purpose lent a unique fervour to the customary words, and he was rewarded by a tingling sensation as energy rose up his spine. Coming to rest in the heart centre, it suffused Rachamim's being with warmth, and his meditation was deep and joyous. When he opened his eyes and looked round, it seemed to him that his own joy was visible on all faces.

After standing to greet the sun, and reciting the morning prayers, the Brothers exchanged the white robes for brown work clothes before dispersing to their various tasks. There were only two hundred Brothers in the Qumran settlement but it was entirely self-sufficient. In spite of the intense heat in this, the lowest-lying region in the country,

Brothers skilled in agriculture cultivated crops irrigated by water trapped in the two cisterns. Others worked in the bakery, the pottery or the Scriptorium, copying scrolls in a fine hand. There was even a loom to weave the clothes worn by the members, white for meals and prayer, brown for work, yellow for pupils. Right from the start of his admission to Qumran, Rachamim had chosen to be a healer, but his first year had been spent learning to read and write good Hebrew, Greek, and Aramaic. When he was familiar with the strict discipline of the Brotherhood, he'd received the white robe of a novice, and started his training as a healer. Together with Menachem and Nissim he'd travelled the length and breadth of the country, tending the sick, bringing comfort and healing. As no Brother might eat any food not prepared by a fellow Essene, they'd relied solely on families of Essenes living in towns and villages, along the way, sometimes going hungry if there were none to be found. Rachamim preferred working in Qumran, where he could enjoy the certainty of simple meals, taken regularly in silence, as a sacrament.

Happy to be home, he walked the short distance from the assembly hall to the House of the Sick, a spacious stone building, set close to the southern reservoir.

There were only three patients. Elisheva, a young woman whose abdomen was grossly distended, and two men afflicted with a skin disorder. Menachem gave brief orders. The nut-brown Nissim with his stubby fingers and love of the soil went happily to the herb garden, where he was to tend the plants damaged by the flash flood of the previous month. That left Rachamim and Ezra to take the two male patients to the Sea of Salt.

They walked over an arid stretch of rocky ground, Ezra still limping slightly, and paused at the edge of the water to strip off their robes. When the patients stood naked except for their loin-cloths, Rachamim took note of their skin. In the cities, any skin disease was branded as potential leprosy, and sufferers kept in seclusion by the priests. If the condition failed to clear after two weeks, the unfortunate patient was declared unclean, and sentenced to live as a leper. Many so-called lepers had been cured at Qumran, though the treatment was often painful.

This is going to hurt," Rachamim said gently, eyeing the rough reddened patches, some crusty with blood. "The waters will sting you now, because of the salt, but try to bear the pain, for the sting is healing.

Supporting the men as their feet slipped on the thick mud of the sea bed, Rachamim and Ezra guided them into the water. As the bitter sea licked at their sores, the patients yelled, trying to struggle free, but Rachamim was firm. "There are purifying elements in this water. They'll make your skin clean, give you new life." The older of the patients looked unconvinced. Nothing lived in this sea, no fish, no plants. Some even called it the Sea of Death, so how could it give life? He turned to make for the shore, but Rachamim held him fast, while Ezra tried to divert him.

"See, you can float on the water," he shouted, lying on his back, toes in the air. "Try it yourself! You'll float, you'll see. But be careful not to splash water into eyes or mouth; it stings, and the taste is bitter."

"Close your eyes," Rachamim poured water from cupped hands on an afflicted cheek. "Remember you are being healed," he added as the man gasped in pain.

Using a special scoop, Ezra collected black mud from the sea bed. Wading cautiously through the heavy waters, he made several trips to the shore with the mud, depositing it in a trough fashioned from the hollowed trunk of a tree.

"The mud, too, has healing properties," Rachamim told his astonished patients, as Ezra carefully plastered their skin with the shiny black stuff. When he'd finished, there was still a little mud left in the trough, and Ezra looked at it thoughtfully. Then he scooped up a thick gob, and daubed it on his own unblemished chest. Rachamim smiled. Bending over, he poked a finger into the mud. Ezra tried to dodge, but Rachamim was too quick, and the mud found its way to Ezra's astonished nose.

One of the patients laughed, then the other, and Rachamim raised his arms. Head thrown back, face lifted to the sky, he began to dance. Moved by joyous energy that surged through his body, he danced a dance of love for the Lord, singing His praises, oblivious of his surroundings, heedless of the lateness of the hour. Infected by his happiness, Ezra and the two men joined in. The black-splashed figures twisted and dipped under the blazing sun, while the pale green waters lapped languid at the shore. The sound of their chanting echoed over the sea, to hang suspended in the pure air, long after they were gone.

Menachem showed no sign of anger or impatience as Rachamim lead the freshly-bathed patients back to the House of the Sick. He greeted them with love, although their lateness had made it impossible for him to attend the Meal of the Pure, held an hour before noon. Rachamim, not yet eligible to attend the Meal, went with Ezra to join the pupils and novices at their meal, but Menachem refused to go with them. "This afternoon we begin the healing of Elisheva," he said. "It seems good to me to fast before it."

Nissim was already at Elisheva's side by the time Rachamim returned to the House of the Sick. While they waited for Menachem, they sat at her side, talking quietly to her anxious husband.

"I've seen this illness many times," Nissim reassured. "By the grace of the Lord, some have been cured."

"Will you give her medicines?"

"I know of some herbs to ease the pain, and these I've already given her. You're feeling less pain now, aren't you, Elisheva?" he asked gently.

"The pain is less, thank you," the sick woman breathed, her sunken dark eyes full of wonder at the herbalist's skill.

"Her limbs are so wasted, yet you only give her grape juice," the husband accused. "She needs food. Shall I go and fetch milk?" He jumped up. "Maybe I'll bring some dates too, to strengthen her."

"Not yet," Nissim said. "Let me explain. We think that the thing which is growing in her abdomen is eating all her food. That's what's making her so thin. If we give milk now, it'll just feed the growth." He smiled kindly. "First the grape juice, to clean and purify the body, and then, when the growth is smaller, we'll give her other foods."

"Will the juice make the growth smaller?"

Nissim shook his head. "No. For that healing is needed. Before we start, we ask the Lord to make her whole. First we ask the Great Healer to forgive the sin which caused the illness, and then we ask for healing energy to come through us, and take away the sickness.

"I hope you can begin soon. We've waited long enough."

"We'll begin right now," said Menachem coming in, followed by Ezra. "Ezra, you stand at her feet." Menachem took his place at Elisheva's head, Rachamim and Nissim at her sides. At a signal from Menachem, Ezra started to chant. His clear note a flute played with the breath of innocence, he chanted the hymn for forgiveness.

> "Yet Thou bringest all the sons of Thy truth
> in forgiveness before Thee,
> To cleanse them of all their faults
> through Thy great goodness,
> And to establish them before Thee
> Through the multitude of Thy mercies
> for ever and ever."

Now the others joined in the hymn, the bells of their voices ringing in the afternoon silence as they sang to the Lord, acknowledging His power.

"Nothing is done without Thee,
  and nothing is known without Thy will."

Even before they had finished, Elisheva was resting quietly. Her husband, soothed by the melody, sat holding her hand.

Menachem's voice, deeper than the rest, announced,

"I will groan with the zither of lamentation
  until iniquity and wickedness are consumed
  and the disease bringing scourge is no more."

Rachamim answered joyously,

"Then will I play on the zither of deliverance
  and the harp of joy,
  and the pipe of praise without end."

As soon as the healing began, Rachamim felt the familiar tingling in his outstretched hands. Although it was late afternoon, the winter sun was still powerful, and the room was hot. He glanced at the others. Nissim's brown face was serious, hands trembling slightly with the healing force. Menachem appeared intent and remote, his hands moving unhurried over Elisheva's head. Only Ezra's sharp little features were flushed as he concentrated. Perhaps he feels the heat too, Rachamim thought. Healers were trained to think of their bodies as hollow reeds through which the breath of the Angel of Healing could flow. If only that breath were not so hot, Rachamim thought impiously, trying not to fidget as sweat trickled down his back.

At home, the breeze would be blowing from the Great Sea as a kinder sun sparkled the waters. Rachamim's nostrils flared, remembering the scent of the ocean spray. How cool the damp sands had felt under bare feet as he walked the shore near his village. Was his father out fishing, the old boat creaking and rocking, fish flapping in the nets? It had been a happy childhood, spent helping with the catch. They sold the fish, still wiggling, to village women standing with baskets on the shore. His mother, kind, warm, loving. Was she feeding yet another at those ample breasts? Did she miss her oldest son? His noisy crowd of brothers, and his sisters, fierce Yehudith and the red-haired twins, did they miss their brother?

With a start, Rachamim came back to the room. Elisheva, twisting in pain as the drug wore off, was searching his face with frightened eyes. Rachamim's compassion surged, and with it came a great force

of energy, which flooded his body, and poured from his hands. Forgetting himself in his patient's need, he joined the current flowing
towards her. He was a tidal wave, engulfing the pain. As the wave
receded, Rachamim reeled in his prize. Triumphant, he felt its stormy
entry into his own belly, felt its fiery fingers clawing at his own
entrails. He exulted at the fierceness of it, and staggered back. Menachem signalled him to withdraw, and the healing session continued
without him.

* * * * *

With the passing of the days, Elisheva made steady progress. A
little colour crept back into the wan cheeks, her expression was peaceful. As the healing energy sapped the strength of the growth, it cow-
ered back, soon to wither and die, flushed from its unwilling host. But
Rachamim no longer saw Elisheva. He no longer went to the Sea with
the patients. There had been a complaint about him from the driver of
a cart sent to fetch the patients from the shore that first day.
Rachamim now worked with Nissim in the herb garden and was not
allowed to visit the House of the Sick. "I'm afraid the incident at the
Sea will delay my admission to full membership," he confided to
Nissim.

"You'll find out soon enough. The Council will sit on the third
day," Nissim said.

* * * * *

The white-robed Brothers filed solemnly into the assembly-room.
No one talked, no one even glanced to right or left, as each Brother
made his way to his prescribed place. At the head of the Assembly sat
the Guardian, flanked by the three priests and the twelve men who
formed the Council of the Community. It was not until every Brother
was seated, and all shuffling had stopped, that the Guardian stood.
Arms folded over his breast, hooded eyes inscrutable under the aqui-
line nose, he saluted the assembled Brothers. The session could now
begin.

At the back of the hall, Rachamim rubbed clammy palms together
as he waited for the judgement. He wasn't unduly worried about his
own case, as he'd already been penalised for his lateness; his anxiety
was for the loss of the donkey, and the implications for his teacher. He
stole a forbidden glance at Menachem under lowered eyelids, but could
tell nothing from that quiet face.

Then the chief scribe was reading the matters for discussion, and Rachamim's heart jumped at the sound of his own name. One of the members had reported the unseemly behaviour of the Brother Rachamim, dancing on the shore, not troubling to conceal his near naked body. Oh, the shame of it! Rachamim suppressed a shiver. What awful penalty awaited him? Certainly he'd lost his chance of admission to full membership. He was asked to stand, and a dreadful fear descended on him as he heard his sentence. Ten day's excommunication. Ten days without food and water. Unthinkable! Even three days absence in the harsh climate of this wilderness was tantamount to a death sentence. Because of the oath forbidding him to accept food or water from strangers, he was going to have to live on leaves or roots, lick the dew from stones. Some had been reprieved and brought back at the point of death, but Rachamim knew he couldn't last that long. He'd go to Jerusalem, he decided, where there was a community of Essenes who might feed him,…if he didn't die of thirst on the way.

But the scribe was reading the second charge, and Rachamim dragged his attention back to the room. Brother Menachem had carelessly disposed of a donkey, the property of the Community, and failed to make any attempt to return the animal.

The sentence passed on Brother Menachem jolted Rachamim from his own misery. Menachem must leave Qumran and search for the donkey. On his return, he must do penance, receiving only a quarter of the food ration for one year.

As the silent Brothers filed out of the Assembly, Rachamim made up his mind. Once outside, and without even asking permission to speak, he approached Menachem . "I'll go with you to find the donkey," he told the older Brother.

"There are no Essenes in Jericho to give you food."

"So be it. Then I will be hungry."

Chapter Fourteen

Caravan

The sun blazed overhead. Leaving the palm-fringed coast where the Great Sea dazzled indigo under an indigo sky, the caravan wound slowly through the rocky landscape of the Sinai desert. Laden camels plodded splay-footed over rocky ground, sparsely dotted with low vegetation. Here and there, a woody acacia tree spread spiky branches, greening the red-brown of the desert landscape. Protective shrouds of cloth wound round the heads and faces of the travellers made speech impossible, and did little to stop a fine drift of sand into mouth and nostrils. The heat dulled Naftali's senses, but not the pain, as memories of Bet-Lehem journeyed with him…the Innkeeper's wife, almost incoherent, her stricken face, her babble. "They killed them all…all the little ones…all the babies. None left. Even the newborn, still in the barn, the mother waiting out the days of her purification." How the woman had sobbed out the story.

"Not even *one* left, out of all the children?" Joseph couldn't accept it.

"We must go to the barn," the Innkeeper had said.

"No!" The Innkeeper's wife screamed.

But the Innkeeper went to the barn, "He should not be left un-buried," he said.

Then Yerusha's face, as her husband came from the barn, carrying the one the soldiers had missed. Her face like a sun breaking through rain clouds, as she folded mother and child to her breast. The child's father had stood with bowed head at the sound of the town's laments borne on wind keen as a knife.

Joseph was practical. What if Herod were to find out that this child was still alive? If the birth in Bet-Lehem had been registered in Jerusalem, Herod had only to search the records. There was no time to waste, the family must rush the child to a safe hiding place. There was a caravan for Egypt leaving from Jerusalem immediately, they should join it, and not come back from Egypt until all danger was past. They must leave at once. But Yerusha had cried out, delaying the departure as she loaded the fugitives with food and wine for the journey, cradling the baby to her breast, unwilling to let him go.

"When we return, we'll come to visit you," the mother Mariam had promised through tears. "Our two children will play together."

* * * * *

Naftali felt strangely comforted by the presence on the journey of the fugitive couple, and sought them out when the caravan rested. A flight to a strange land, carrying a tiny infant, would have daunted the strongest of mothers, but this one stayed so calm, and he enjoyed watching her. Her husband, Joseph, an older man, confided that they hoped to stay at a village of the Jews he knew of, near Alexandria, and wait there until it was safe to return home.

"I'll come to look for you after I've bought the cloth I need for the Temple," Naftali promised, watching as Mariam tended her baby. She sat in the shade of a huge rock, bathing the small limbs in water from a copper pan. Such capable hands, he thought, suddenly envying the child. What would it be like to be her child and be tended by her? A laughable fantasy, he rebuked himself, shaking his head to clear it of the daydream. Water splashed over the sand as Mariam emptied the copper vessel and went off to prepare food for herself and her husband.

After dark the desert air was coldly clean. Under a canopy of stars, the pregnant moon nightly birthed a myriad beams, lighting wind-sculpted rocks that cast fantastic shadows. Relieved of their burdens, the camels rested standing or lying in a half circle. Precious bales of wool, vats of wine, and bundles of balsam, were stacked within the circle, guarded by a strong servant.

"Tonight you'll come and eat with us," said Ahab, the tall young leader of the caravan. "There's good wine tonight," he promised, taking Naftali by the arm, and drawing him over to where the drovers had kindled a fire. Naftali had small interest in the traders and the rough camel drovers, but grudgingly allowed himself to be lead to join them.

There were two other traders; Shem an older man with thinning hair and straggling beard, and Daniel, robust and curly haired. They squatted round the fire, warming themselves, talking, laughing and eating.

"How many children have you fathered, Naftali?" Daniel asked, his face flushed by fire and wine.

"I've no children."

"Well, you're still young. When you've finished trading in Egypt, hurry home, and give your wife a good son."

"I have no wife."

Everybody stopped eating to look at him.

"How did she die?" Ahab asked.

"I never married."

Incredulous silence, and the drovers' unbelieving faces.

"Tomorrow we'll start early," kindly Ahab said loudly to cover his embarrassment; but an uneasy silence had fallen.

Shem articulated into his beard, "An Israelite child is born, he is circumcised, he reaches manhood and he marries. The Lord said, 'Be fruitful and multiply.' So tell us, Naftali, why did you defy Him?"

One of the drovers grunted in disdain, "In my village, an unmarried man is held to be no better than a murderer."

"We aren't in your village now, and mind your tongue," Ahab rebuked. "I've heard tell of certain among the Essenes who live in community at Qumran. These men don't marry. Yet they are pious Jews."

"Well, he's not one of them," Daniel muttered. "He's a trader, just like me, even though he wears the clothes of a Sadducee."

"Those Essenes don't marry as they want to devote all their time to the Lord," Naftali said, "It was what I intended to do. It was the reason I didn't marry." But it was pointless trying to explain to these people, and he got up. Engrossed in thought, shoulders hunched, he tracked to the outcrop of rocks. This was the place where Mariam had bathed her baby. As he sat down Naftali noticed a tracery of delicate blue flowers, splashed over the barren ground. Strange, he thought, how even a small amount of water can bring out flowers so swiftly.

He didn't know how long he'd sat there when he heard it; Mariam's voice, clear and sweet, floating in the moonlit air.

"Sleep, my son, God's precious gift,
The moon she bows before you
Stars will form a pretty crown,
And angels bright adore you."

Naftali pulled his rough blanket around him, and stretched out to sleep while Mariam sang on,

"Sleep, my son, and close your eyes,
Your mother she is near,
And while you sleep will watch and pray,
And keep you far from fear."

"She was so young," Naftali was to tell Joseph later, "How could I have felt she was my mother? I felt she sang to me, as well to her child. How can that be? How could I have felt that I, too, was her child?"

Chapter Fifteen

Frail Blossom

Motherhood suited Sarah. Her cheeks glowed pink, her glossy braid bounced under a festive veil as she walked to Tamar's house. Leaving Devorah to tend the twins, she made straight for Tamar's room, eyes shining with anticipation. Remembering her own betrothal to Joseph, how excited she'd felt, she guessed Tamar must be feeling the same. As she hurried in she was greeted by Abishag in a new blue tunic, her hair still damp from the washing she'd endured.

"Abishag, why the solemn face? Don't you like your new clothes?"

Abishag gestured helplessly to Tamar.

Tamar was sitting with her back to the room, staring out onto the small courtyard. She didn't turn as Sarah came in.

Sarah crossed quickly to her, her smile dying. Sinking to her knees, she clasped the cold hands.

"Oh, Tamar, what is it my love? Are you so afraid?" Tamar didn't answer, but her eyes glittered expressively. She's going to cry, Sarah thought anxiously, stroking the tangled hair as she reassured her friend. "It's all right, Tamar, little dove, you'll see. He will be beautiful, your betrothed. I've heard he's young and healthy, from a very good family. I know you'll grow to love him; please don't be afraid."

Tamar still didn't answer, her hands limp in her lap. Sarah, puzzled, got to her feet.

"Are you ill, Tamar? I'll fetch your mother."

"No!"

"Then won't you tell me what's the matter? You can talk to me. Are you fasting? Perhaps a little milk to sustain you?"

"I'm not hungry."

"Shall I help you dress? You are surely not planning to wear your shift to the ceremony?" Sarah picked up a comb, and started to comb the long curls. Tamar sat unresisting, head bowed. She's more like a mourner at a funeral than a bride, Sarah thought. Perhaps Abishag knows something? She raised enquiring eyebrows at Abishag.

Abishag said, "Tamar has been sad for many days. Her new robe is here, but she hasn't even looked at it." She lifted it from the bed, holding it up proudly for Sarah to see. Woven of the finest wool, it was coloured a deep violet and bordered with gold, with two golden girdles to hold it in place. For Tamar's head, there was a gauzy pink veil, and a coronet of fragile almond blossom.

"Oh, Tamar, it's so beautiful!" Sarah cried "I wonder what you'll wear for the wedding? I can't imagine any other dress as lovely as this one."

"We've plenty of time to think about that." Rachel said, hurrying in wearing festive clothes, the dark red silk swamping her faded Eastern beauty. "Although the wedding date has already been decided," she continued proudly. "Ephraim's family doesn't want to wait the full year, so we've set the date for Marchesvan." She greeted Sarah, brushing her cheek briefly, while speaking to Tamar. "Don't look so sad, daughter, it's a day for rejoicing, not for tears. A gift has come from your betrothed. I can't guess what it can be, but it's sure to cheer you up. Go and bring it, Abishag. it's in the entrance hall. Tamar, after you've seen it, please start to dress. We can't keep the groom waiting."

I don't like her, thought Sarah. Hasn't she noticed Tamar is unhappy? Doesn't she see her pain? Perhaps she thinks it's natural for a virgin to feel distress on the eve of her betrothal. Still, Rachel has always been strange, she reflected, remembering how uncaring she'd been when Tamar's singing birds had died. "They're only birds," she'd said, "throw them away, Abishag, and do stop crying Tamar, you're a grown woman not a child. A grown woman never cries." Maybe it was because Rachel was from India, a barbaric land where they worshipped idols with the heads of elephants. Sarah had even heard tell that mothers put their daughters' little fingers in boiling water, to get the girls used to bearing pain without flinching. The shrivelled fingers must have been a constant threat of fiery death on the dead husband's funeral bier. Dreadful. Sarah shuddered. At least Rachel was of the Jewish faith, even if she did often behave like an unfeeling heathen. Poor Tamar with such a mother. Sarah's eyes softened, remembering how understanding her own mother had been at her betrothal to Joseph. She'd explained to Sarah that though betrothal was considered as binding as marriage, a bride need not lie with her betrothed immediately. If she preferred, it was within her rights to wait right up to the time she was married. Maybe Rachel hadn't told this to Tamar?

Sarah was about to question her friend on this delicate matter, when Abishag came in with a basket, which she set at Tamar's feet.

"Aren't you going to open it?" Sarah asked.

"You do it," said Tamar dully.

Sarah's fingers fumbled with the clasp on the lid. "Whatever can it be?" she muttered.

"Oh!" she jumped back, "What is it?"

Abishag peered into the basket, exclaiming in pleasure, "It's a little animal! It's so pretty." She put tentative hands inside, lifted a small furry body, and placed it carefully on Tamar's lap. The creature had green eyes, pricked-up ears, a wisp of a tail, and silky fur. Tamar gasped. "What is it? What can it be?" She looked in wonder at the tiny animal, which clung to her shift with sharp little claws.

"I think it's a young cat," Sarah said, "I've seen some grown ones. Joseph said they have plenty of them in Egypt, they even make graven images of them."

Tamar put the cat on the ground, where it quickly found its feet. A swift paw tapped a fallen bauble, and it pounced.

Tamar's sad eyes lit with pleasure. "Oh, it's wonderful! What shall we feed it Sarah? What can it eat?"

"It's a baby. It needs milk."

"Abishag, quickly, bring milk," Tamar ordered, scooping up the kitten and pressing her cheek to the warm body.

"What shall I call him?"

"How do you know it's a male?"

They searched the pink belly. "It's a female," Sarah pronounced, "not a foreskin in sight." She giggled. "Soon it will be Queen Esther's Festival. Why don't you call her Malka, queen?

"No, not Malka."

"Well, Adar, then. Since this is the start of the month of Adar."

"No, I don't like Adar, "Tamar said vehemently. "Even though the almond trees are in blossom". She glanced unhappily at her veil.

Sarah put her arms around her. "Come Tamar, aren't we friends? Can't you tell me what's making you unhappy? I won't tell anyone, you can trust me, I promise."

"Lately I have had no issue of blood."

"Is that all? Well that's nothing to worry about. I too had no issue at the time of my betrothal. Mother said it was because I was afraid and nervous at the time, not knowing how it would be...lying for the first time with a man."

"Really? Are you sure, Sarah? It happens because of agitation? I have been quite agitated lately."

"Really. I'm sure. After I'd seen Joseph, and became calmer, knowing that he was kind, the flow returned; though it took some months. Didn't you ask your mother? She's very skilled in these matters."

"No, I didn't ask, and please don't tell her Sarah," Tamar pleaded.

"I promised, didn't I? I won't tell anyone. Did you get the milk, Abishag?"

Abishag put down the bowl she carried. "Here you are, little mi-mi. Look, she drinks with her tongue," she squealed.

Tamar laughed aloud. "Yes, she is Mimi. I'll dress now," she said.

* * * * *

Sarah studied the groom as the priest intoned the blessing. Not much older than Tamar. He seemed shy. Unlikely to want to consummate the union until they married. Tamar would be calmer by then.

Ephraim ben Manasseh had short red hair, cut in the Roman style, and the pale complexion so often seen with that hair colour. Light blue eyes flickered under sandy lashes. Nervous. He'll soon get over it, Sarah decided, smug in her full seventeen years. They'll play together like two children. Tamar looks happier. Could that be the kitten under her veil? She's like a little Indian princess with her new toy. Sarah took Joseph's arm, mingling with the guests, exchanging greetings, talking, laughing. Joseph smiled at the surprise on the faces of the twins, sucking butter from a proffered finger.

The festive honey cakes were still sweet on lips red from heady wine when the music started. Flute and drum and tambourine, the musicians played a merry tune. Seduced by the sound, the dancing circles formed; the ring of men with a laughing Ephraim; Tamar swept up by the women. As she whirled, petals spilled from the frail almond blossom crown, catching in loosened hair under the lifting veil.

Too short-lived, those flowers, Sarah thought; jasmine buds last longer.

Chapter Sixteen

Shulamith

They'd been told to go, and they left that night. No time for preparations, and indeed nothing to prepare, for they took nothing with them. Striding along the moonlit path that lead northwards to Jericho, Rachamim struggled with his fear.

"Have no fear," said Menachem, "Whatever happens is the will of the Lord."

How does he know I'm afraid? And what if it's the will of the Lord that we get attached by robbers?

"We have nothing to steal," Menachem said calmly, surprising Rachamim again as he heard his thought.

The Brothers had no provision for this journey, no change of clothing, no blanket. Even the small hatchet they usually carried to dig the hole for the relief of their needs had been left behind, for all these things were the property of the Community.

When Rachamim had first come to Qumran, he had brought a meagre sum, all his hard-working family could provide. Menachem, however, had brought considerable wealth. But now, Rachamim thought, we have nothing.

Painful ideas continued to prick him like so many sharp-pointed thorns. What if we die of hunger before we find the donkey? What is it like to hunger and thirst till you die? I don't want to die yet! Not so young. I want to live…and work…and pray.

"It seems we're not going to die of hunger and thirst just yet, Brother Rachamim," Menachem suddenly interrupted these dire thoughts.

"How did you guess what I was thinking?"

Menachem avoided the question. "Look over there. Don't you see? Ezra is coming from his house even now."

Rachamim could see nothing. The small houses where married members lived, slept in the shadow of the craggy cliffside. Nothing stirred. Only a few rock-rabbits, attracted by crops on the sloping ter-races, hopped quietly, searching for food.

He's mistaken, no one is there, Rachamim decided, looking at Menachem fondly. Menachem had been his teacher for two years. The older Brother had come to the fishing village where Rachamim's family lived when Rachamim was still a child. At that time there had been a serious outbreak of fever in the land, and the Brothers in white had travelled far and wide, bringing medicines and healing the sick. From the start, the young Rachamim had been drawn to the healers and he'd spent all his time in their company. The boy had listened entranced as they talked of the glories of the Nameless One, and His wonderful healing works. Rachamim had known, young as he was, that this was what he wanted; a life of service to the Lord, and a knowledge of healing like the Brothers had.

His family had not laughed at the strange idea when he told them. Although they themselves were fishermen, and expected their son to carry on the family tradition, they'd sensed the power of the unassuming Essenes, and were filled with gratitude for healing they'd received. They'd finally agreed that if Rachamim still felt as he did after his Bar Mitzvah, his initiation into manhood, at age twelve, he was free to apply to join the Community. Miraculously, Menachem had returned to the village shortly after Rachamim's Bar Mitzvah, and when he left, Rachamim went with him.

After he'd been at Qumran for a year, and had learned to read and write, Menachem had undertaken his training as a healer. Infinitely patient, calm and wise, the older man had taught far more than how to care for the sick. Even when helping him to understand and abide by the ideals of the Qumran Community, Menachem had imposed no dogma on him, allowing Rachamim to come to the truth from his own experience. He'd been careful to foster his pupil's own unique way of transmitting healing energy, a way which differed greatly from his own. If Rachamim had fears and doubts, it had been Menachem who had understood, comforted and encouraged him. He's well named, Rachamim thought, Menachem 'he who comforts.' But what comfort can he give me now, on this foolish quest?

"There is Ezra now," Menachem said, pointing.

Three figures emerged from deep shadow at the side of one of the houses, Ezra and his foster-parents, Dinah and Yoav, hurrying towards them.

"Shalom," Menachem greeted.

"Peace and blessings." The little group halted shyly.

"Ezra has something to say," said Yoav, and Menachem nodded permission.

"We couldn't let you go without provisions. So we brought you some of our own. Will you take them?"

As Menachem smiled acceptance, Yoav said, "Ezra, fetch them from the house."

Nimble as the gazelles which graced this rocky land, Ezra bounded over the track, returning with his arms full. "Here is water." He handed a full skin to each of the Brothers.

"And you can re-fill them yourselves when you get to Jericho," Yoav said, "I hear there is abundant water there."

"Here is food," Dinah said. "It's only barley bread, and some goat's cheese, but there are dried figs, and almonds too."

Ezra flung himself on Rachamim, clinging tightly. "You *will* come back soon, my teacher, come soon."

Rachamim pulled the curly head to his chest. "Ezra, we'll come back soon, and we'll all work together with the patients. Be brave, and help Nissim while we're gone." He patted the thin shoulders. Then turning to Yoav, he asked, "How did you know we were leaving Qumran tonight?"

"Ezra heard."

"But Ezra was at home with you."

"He has the gift," Dinah said proudly.

I seem to be the only one who hasn't, Rachamim thought, feeling a little saddened at his own poverty.

"You have other gifts, Rachamim," Menachem said softly, "and now we must go on."

* * * * *

After the arid landscape of the wilderness they had passed through, the lush vegetation of the oasis of Jericho was a pleasant sight. Here the wealthy spent the winters, as the low-lying city enjoyed hot sun-shine, in sharp contrast to Jerusalem's colder windy climate. The Brothers skirted one of Herod's three winter palaces, whose colon-naded courts overlooked the pleasant waters of the wadi Qelt. Courtiers walked in sunken gardens rich with palm trees and flowering shrubs, while nearby orchards lent cool green shade.

The pair stopped to rest. After bathing as best they could in the waters of the wadi, they ate sparingly of the food they'd been given, and stretched out to sleep in the shade.

It was late in the afternoon when they woke. "We'll go first to the market-place," Menachem said, and ask where we can find Amnon's uncle, Aaron ben David."

"There must be so many with that common name" Rachamim muttered, his feeling of hopelessness growing as they walked into the busy market-place. Jews, Arabs, Phoenicians, Romans, Greeks, thronged the narrow streets and crowded bazaars. Rachamim had never been in a city so large. The market was a moving mosaic of courtiers in rich robes, toga'ed Romans and their wealthy wives, elaborate hair-styles studded with gold, pious Jews with fringed shawls, poorer citizens in faded clothes. Beggars held out blackened hands for alms, some displaying maimed or crippled limbs. And everywhere there were the cries, a cacophony of street noises, as eager pedlars shouted their wares; babbling voices speaking different tongues. It was like being in a raucous dream. As they jostled through the crowd, Rachamim thought longingly of the silence and peace of Qumran, the sweet music of the evening prayer.

"Aaron ben David?" asked a stall-holder, a burly man presiding over a mound of cheeses. "No, I don't know him. Try the olive vendor." But the olive-vendor had not heard of the family of ben David. Scooping a ladle into olives bobbing blackly in brine, he offered them to the Brothers, shrugging good-humouredly when they refused. They met with the same response from the other stalls they visited. A peasant woman selling fine wheat-bread, a farmer with apples so beautiful the mouth watered looking at them, the sandal-maker and the wine merchant, none had heard of Aaron ben David.

"Too many Jews called Aaron," said the fruit vendor. "Go to the wells, and ask the women. Women know all the latest gossip. Maybe they can tell you of a new-comer to the town, a nephew of Aaron ben David."

The well was a long way from the town, and the Brothers were forced to leave the market and take a path which wound through a large tract of open ground. Hot, tired and thirsty, they trudged along in the heat of a sultry afternoon. Air hung heavy under dark rain cloud, and the few strangers they met on the way hurried purposefully homewards. When at last they reached the well, none of the women there could help them, though they questioned many. They were turning to leave when a woman, friendlier than the rest, asked them where they would stay that night.

"You are welcome to shelter with my husband and I," she said, "if you will come to a humble home."

Rachamim was relieved when Menachem accepted. The pair filled their water-skins, and set off with the woman Bat-Sheva to her home. As they walked, the rain started. The first large drops spattered the ground, slowly at first, then fast and insistent, churning the dust to thick mud. They reached the house, filthy robes flapping wetly round their ankles, and stooped under the low doorway to find themselves in a dark airless room. Bat-Sheva lit a solitary lamp.

"Please sit down," she indicated the earth floor, "I'll make a hot broth. My husband will come soon, and we can eat together."

Rachamim wished they didn't have to refuse; a hot soup would have been welcome, but Menachem was already explaining courteously why they couldn't share, though he thanked Bat-Sheva for her offer.

Rachamim tried not to shiver as he huddled damply to pray. The evening prayer seemed interminable tonight. The cooking fire smoked and stung his eyes, and the enticing smell of stewing vegetables made him drool. They had eaten nothing except a few almonds since the morning. He got up dejected. Meditation was impossible. How could he meditate when he was so cold, so hungry? Berating himself for his failure to rise above the body's demands, he moved nearer to the fire to dry his clothes, leaving Menachem to meditate alone.

The rain continued all night, plopping through the poor roof, targeting now a foot, now a leg, and finally sizzling into the fire, which died a smoky death. Bat-Sheva had no spare blanket to offer, but Menachem slept calmly, wrapped in a blanket of peace, while Rachamim kept unwilling vigil.

He must have dosed though, he thought, opening his eyes to faint light filtering through the one mean window. There was no sign of Bat-Sheva or her husband. He stumbled stiffly outside. In the dirty communal courtyard Rachamim found a rudimentary privy, then washed himself as best he could from a trough filled with fresh rain water. Facing the sun, he stood to recite the morning prayers. It'll be better today, he thought. The rain has stopped, we're sure to find Amnon today, and we'll take the donkey back to Qumran.

But it was not to be. There was an unnatural flush on Menachem's face when he woke.

"We'll go to the wadi first," he told Rachamim, bathe ourselves, and wash our clothes.

"And Amnon, and the donkey?"

"Later."

They ate the last of the almonds sitting on the bank of the wadi. The sun beat down, drying their robes, but Menachem shivered in the heat.

This day's quest seemed as fruitless as the previous, but just as Rachamim was beginning to despair of ever finding Aaron, they met a man in the market who gave them some hope.

"I heard you asking the carpenter for Aaron ben David. I know a man of that name. He lives south of the town, near my house. I'm David, and I can take you there when I return if you will wait until I finish my work. As for a nephew with a donkey, I can't tell, but you can ask Aaron yourselves."

* * * * *

The house appeared empty. Rachamim hammered on the closed door, but no one answered.

"Knock again."

Hearing the noise, a man in brown came from the house next door. "Are you looking for Aaron? Well, he's not at home. I'm Simon, his neighbour."

"Do you know when Aaron will return?"

"He said he'd be back in a few days. He's gone to Jerusalem."

"Was his nephew with him?"

"Who are you, that you want to know so much?"

Rachamim explained.

"Aaron is an old man, and his legs are weak; so when his nephew came with the donkey, it was like a gift from the Lord! For years Aaron has talked of his wish to visit the Temple and offer sacrifice there. So he used the donkey to ride to Jerusalem, and his nephew went with him."

"We'll have to wait," said Rachamim.

"You are welcome to shelter under my roof," said Simon

It was a spacious house, clean and cool, and Simon was friendly. "Will you share my bread?"

It was painful to refuse. Rachamim's healthy young body demanding food, his stomach rumbling emptily.

"I have never met stranger customs," Simon said. "This food is ritually pure and clean, so why the oath not to eat? Why this hunger that you can't satisfy?"

"We may only take food from others of our community," Rachamim said, hoping Menachem would explain. But Menachem sat quiet and distant, shivering in the warm splash of sunlight coming from a window. He had said little all day.

Rachamim crossed to his side, searching the beloved face with trained eyes.

"May I?"

Menachem obediently held out his hand. The pulse was erratic, the skin burning to the touch. Fever!

Herbs. He must find herbs. Where did they grow in these unfamiliar parts? He wasn't even sure he could identify the necessary plants if he saw them. Now he regretted not paying better attention to Nissim as he tried to teach him in the herb garden at Qumran. He began to mutter names under his breath, as if the saying of them could bring them near; Achillea, marvah, allium, hyssop, repeating them over and over.

Menachem spoke with difficulty, "Try to find herbs. I will rest here."

"How can I leave you alone?"

"I'll stay with him," Simon offered. "There is a widow who grows herbs. It's far from here, but I'll tell you how to go."

The sun was still high as Rachamim walked, light-headed with hunger, concern for Menachem driving him on. When at last he came to the widow's house, he was relieved to find her at home. She stood in the doorway, a slight figure in a blue robe.

"Yes, I am Shulamith. Do you need herbs?"

"Herbs for a fever."

"Is it for yourself?"

Rachamim shook his head.

"I have herbs for fever, dried and ready to infuse. I can prepare you some. Come inside and rest a while.

"Thank you. I'll wait outside."

She shrugged. "At least let me bring you some bread and wine. You look tired."

Refusing, he kept his eyes on her feet. Small slim feet, wide blue skirts. He felt faint and dazed, but staggered back from the protective arm she put out to steady him.

"Please sit down and rest."

"I must get back to my Brother."

"First you rest, while I prepare the herbs."

He sat wearily, looking up into a young face, a moon of beauty, the eyes dark as his own, full of concern. He wanted to thank her, but instead he asked if she would kindly use the water he'd drawn himself from the well.

"I have my own water, freshly drawn," she said.

How could he tell this young woman that water drawn by any but themselves was considered impure by the Brothers? Her spotless clothing and modest demeanour seemed to him the essence of purity.

"Please use this water for the infusion," he said.

Shulamith took the proffered water-skin and he watched as she turned and went into the house, moving noiselessly.

The minutes crept by. Unable to relax, he took to pacing up and down. What was she doing? How long did it take to infuse a few herbs? It was getting late, the sun would set, darkness fall and he'd never find the way back. Menachem needed him. He edged towards the door, grew bolder, and stepped inside, calling her name. But there was no answer. He looked around. By the light of two carefully placed oil lamps, he made out several large pottery jars, filled with dried plants, their spiky shadows patterning the walls. There was a curtain at the back of the room, and he thought she must be out there, though he heard nothing.

"Shulamith," he called again, parting the curtain to reveal a walled garden. There were neat beds of herbs edged with budding bushes, a circular oven, and a cooking stove on the ground over a fire-pit. Shulamith crouched over a steaming pot, was decanting pale yellow liquid into a jar. Seeing Rachamim, she straightened and adjusted her veil, face flushed from the fire, tiny tendrils of hair curling damply.

"It's ready," she said. "We can take it to your Brother now."

"We?"

"I'll come too. I know all the quick ways. Besides, I can look at the patient, and see if there is something else I can do for him."

She reached for a woven basket, and placed the jar carefully inside.

"I'll carry it," Rachamim offered.

Shulamith picked up one of the lighted lamps, and a spare phial of oil, and they set off together, walking as quickly as they could.

She stole a glance at Rachamim. "You think I look young, don't you, for a widow?"

"Yes, that's true."

"Well, I'm fully thirteen, a grown woman."

He didn't reply. She smelled of herbs and fresh washed linen. He mustn't look at her.

"Some say I have the evil eye."

"How can that be?"

"My husband died on the night of the wedding ceremony. He was an old man with children of his own by his first wife. Children older than I. They said I should think myself lucky, an orphan like me, marrying a rich man." She paused. "It was because he was old, an old man, and I was young. He wanted so much to... he wanted..."

"I understand," Rachamim said quickly, interrupting.

"Do you?" she laughed. "I don't think so. How could a celibate from a religious community possibly understand?"

"I'm from a large family."

"Ah, well, I have no family, and his children think I have the evil eye and avoid me. Luckily I have the house, I grow the herbs, I lack for nothing." But she sounded sad.

She wants a child to love, Rachamim guessed, a baby to put to her breast. He tore his eyes away.

They could hear the sound of Menachem's coughing even before they reached the house. "I'm coming, I'm coming," Rachamim shouted, quickening his pace, bursting unceremoniously into the room.

"I brought medicine." Cradling Menachem's thin body in his arms, he drew him to a sitting position and held the jar to the parched lips, urging him to drink. A pleasant scent of balsam came from the potion, so why was Menachem refusing, looking at Shulamith through fevered eyes?

"I drew the water for the infusion myself," Rachamim reassured. Menachem drank a little then, swallowing with difficulty, and sank back exhausted, eyes closed.

Rachamim started a healing chant, the hoarse notes trickling in thin mockery of the usual flowing melody. As he stretched out his hands to heal, the familiar feeling of love and compassion swelled strongly in him, pervading his body. He waited for the healing energy to pass from him to Menachem, but nothing happened. He stood mute, patient, praying in the dark room, the silence broken only by Menachem's rasping breathing, his racking cough.

Simon came in and lighted a lamp. He greeted Shulamith, then respectfully withdrew to prepare his evening meal, and still Rachamim stood. At last, Menachem summoned strength, raised a hand in the familiar signal, and Rachamim stopped. Exhausted, dizzy with hunger, and bewildered, he slumped frustrated to the ground, slow impotent tears welling in his tired eyes. He was only dimly aware of a hand over his hair, a butterfly caress in a scented breeze, as Shulamith took her leave.

Morning brought no improvement. Menachem tossed, delirious, uttered fragments of prayer, chanted broken praises, and when Rachamim tried to help him drink, the medicine trickled from his mouth and down his beard. I need to draw more water, Rachamim thought. In his desperation, he didn't stop to pray, but hurried to the well, panting the morning prayer as he went. It was very early, and only the morning birds were awake. He envied them their carefree song. If Amnon doesn't return today, Menachem will surely die, he mourned, praying for a miracle.

But Amnon did not return, and in the evening, Rachamim broke his vow.

"I need bread, to be strong again, and heal my Brother," he told Simon.

Trying not to think of the consequences, he tore into the food Simon offered, and when he was satisfied, tried once again to channel the healing energy. Holding his hands over Menachem, he prayed with renewed fervour, imploring help from the Angel of Healing. In vain. Instead of compassion, hopelessness swept through his body. I have lost Menachem, he despaired, and now I've lost Qumran. I'm unworthy of ever taking my place there again. I have lost all I love.

At last, Menachem slept, breathing with difficulty, a ragged quivering breath. Rachamim took the burning hand gently in both of his, reciting the prayer for the dying. He didn't even hear the door opening till Amnon was right inside, taking in the scene in an agony of disbelief.

Chapter Seventeen.

A Special Child

The cloth merchant's sweating servant pulled out yet one more bale of precious material, and draped it over a stand for Naftali to inspect.

But Naftali shook his head. "No, no, too flimsy," and the rejected cloth joined the growing pile of heaped materials in the corner. Green, gold, purple, blue, each colour beckoned seductively, but none had yet found favour in Naftali's eyes. Tired and hungry, he demanded irritably, "I need something very special. Nothing you've shown me so far is at all suitable."

The cloth merchant had been waiting greedily for this moment. "There is a cloth…but perhaps it is not suitable. Perhaps it's too costly. Very special…but maybe you wouldn't like it. You should look at the blue again." He tugged out a rich blue from the bottom of the heap.

"No, no, I already told you I wouldn't take the blue. It's too plain. Where is this other cloth you talk of?"

"Will you think again about the green? A very unusual colour, dyed with a plant extract."

Naftali glared at him. "Show me the other."

The servant was dispatched to the storage room, and as soon as Naftali saw the cloth, he knew it was perfect. A rich, dark crimson with an intricate design of lilies woven into it, it was a field of splendour. Such beauty. He pictured it in the Temple, perhaps even veiling the Holy of Holies, and decided it was worthy.

But delight and relief soon turned to stupefaction when he heard the price. So many gold talents! Much more than the generous sum Joseph had entrusted to him. He offered the merchant half the sum, and the slow bargaining began. It was a long tiresome afternoon.

Finally Naftali got up. "I'll have to look for another place to buy."

At these time-honoured words, the merchant capitulated. He quoted the sum he had originally intended to receive, and Naftali wearily agreed. The cloth would cost him all Joseph's money, and most of his own, and he realised he wouldn't be able to stay in Egypt as long as he'd intended.

"Pack it very carefully," he warned. "Have it ready when I come tomorrow."

Solace

Joseph, greetings,

The material for the curtains is bought, and I sit in this miserable hot caravanserai, waiting for Ahab to lead the caravan back to Jerusalem. Ahab's been instructed to guard the material with his life! I know you'll approve of my choice of colour and texture. I didn't spare the cost, but I think it is worth it.

How I would love to go with this caravan, and be with you all again; for I am filled with longing for your company, and restless for home. The Egyptians are friendly enough, but a strange people. So many statues: gods with heads of birds or dogs, gods with pot-bellies and exposed breasts; how can they worship such things? I've seen it all before, but I still feel as if I'm in a dream. Daily I expect to wake up, and find myself at home, sitting with you at the Inn. Fresh clean air, fresh clean food. Here, I'm forced to exist on dishes of beans, which I must admit are excellent, but I have small appetite so far from home. Now that the transaction is over, and our little family safely arrived in Alexandria, I find myself with too much time to think about Tamar. Is she betrothed? Does she once again laugh with Sarah in her room, eating sweets and talking like maidens at the well?

Once the caravan is safely on its way, I shall go to a village of our own people, where I can stay. It won't be for as long as I intended, as I have spent most of the money I brought with me. I know I could ask you to send more, but I am torn between longing to be home, and dread. The longing is stronger, so I'll return when the money is finished.

I shall spend the Passover here, but not as a prisoner in this land of Egypt. Rather as a prisoner of circumstance. No blood of the lamb on the door-post can buy my freedom from regrets. I look into the future, and worldly happiness seems as unattainable as the moon. Perhaps there is a truer joy for me in a life of celibacy and prayer, and for that I shall enquire of the Essenes at Qumran when I return.

Will you greet my family for me? And Sarah, and your two lovely sons?

Peace and blessings,
   Naftali

* * * * *

Arriving at the village shortly before nightfall, Naftali hurried through the streets. It was the eve of the Sabbath, and he felt a pressing need to immerse himself in the mikvah, and join in the prayers.

The House of Prayer, built of stone, stood a little apart from the rectangular houses of sun-dried brick. Several men were already converging on it, some gathering outside to talk in low tones. By the time Naftali had bathed in the mikvah and changed into a clean robe from his pack, the prayers had already started. Wrapped in his striped prayer shawl, Naftali began to intone the prayer for the Sabbath, but after a few minutes, he stopped, puzzled. The worshippers were chanting different prayers, unfamiliar to him. Where was the welcome for the Sabbath Bride, where the expectant pause as the sky was scanned for the first stars, the heralds of the holy day? Yet these people looked like Jews. Perhaps living in exile had made them forget the ways of the Children of Israel? At home, people searched the congregation for an unknown face, eager to invite a stranger to the house to share the Sabbath meal. Naftali waited with growing unease, but nobody approached him. Yet they seemed kind and pleasant enough, glancing in his direction, smiling to acknowledge the presence of a stranger in their midst.

The ceremony over, the worshippers formed a little knot, nodding in his direction. They appeared to be discussing him, giving instructions to a child, who came over to where he was sitting.

"Peace be with you," said the boy.

"Peace be with you," Naftali answered, studying the child by the dim light of the oil lamps. A long-haired child, in a coarse yellow tunic.

"My name is David. What are you called?"

"Greetings, David. My name is Naftali. Are you sent to fetch me?"

"You are to come to the house of Esther and Gidean, and I'm to bring you. Will you come with me?"

"Are they your parents, Esther and Gidean?"

"My parents? No, they are old people, who have room in their house for guests. There are too many children in our house, it's quite full!" He took Naftali's hand in his small firm one. "Come."

Naftali stooped to enter the low doorway, and was pleased to see the house was much the same as houses he'd visited in Judaea or Galilee. A woman sat in shadow on the raised platform, her copper hair burnished by fire-light coming from beneath a bubbling pot.

"Peace and blessings," a pleasant-faced man welcomed, crossing his arms over his chest, the right one over the left.

"Peace and Sabbath blessings." Naftali returned the unfamiliar salute.

"Not the Sabbath," an older grey-haired woman said. "I am Esther, my husband is Gidean. We are pleased you will be our guest. You must stay as long as you need, and be welcome. The food will be ready soon."

Naftali thanked her, uncertain what to say. What kind of Jews were these? How could they prepare food on the Sabbath, the day of rest, and then deny it was the Sabbath?

Gidean noticed his perplexity. "We are Essenes, and we celebrate the Sabbath on what is for you the fourth day."

"It's fortunate you came today, and not on the Sabbath," the impish David grinned. "There's no food on the Sabbath. Only for children!"

"I didn't know."

"A woman's got to rest too," Esther said, "so we don't serve food."

"We rest our stomachs once a week," Gidean added, motioning to Naftali to sit.

Esther brought water to wash his hands, and he was relieved to hear her intone a familiar prayer.

"I'll bring food," she said, "but first you shall meet Michal." She gestured towards the woman sitting in the shadows, who raised her head, turning the milky eyes of the blind in his direction.

"Welcome to our house," she said, her voice low and warm, "You've come to visit on the same day as the baby." She indicated a shawled bundle in her lap. Then, sensing his confusion, she laughed, "Come and see, come and see. David, bring our guest here."

As David pulled Naftali towards the platform, Michal opened the shawl covering the child, and Naftali gasped in amazement.

"It's the child Yeshua, the son of Mariam," he said.

"So you've met Mariam? Yes, it's Mariam's small Yeshua, and she brought him for me to hold." She traced the small face lovingly with gentle fingers. "Isn't he the most beautiful child that ever was?"

The infant turned sky-blue eyes on Naftali.

"Sit down," Michal patted the blanket beside her, "Would you like to hold him a little?"

Carefully Naftali took the warm bundle. He had only once held a baby before, one of Joseph's little ones, but this one felt different, because the small limbs were unbound. He could see the hands, the little nails, like transparent sea-shells. The infant put a diminutive thumb in his mouth, cuddled contentedly in Naftali's arms, and closed his eyes. Naftali bent his head to breathe in the fragrance of silky hair, and the baby scent of the small warm cheek. He was afraid to move, and sat quietly, holding the child.

As he sat, a sense of well being spread gently through his body. A warm glow, coming from the region of his heart, wrapped first himself, then the child, then the whole room. Naftali seemed to be disappearing into it. He tried to think, to find an explanation, to reassure himself he was in the room, and safe in his body; but where *was* his body? Where was he? Who was thinking these thoughts that came slower and slower, refusing to obey him? He tried to hold on to his mind, but all thought had fled, and in the great silence of his inner being, he found himself in an ocean of peace.

Someone was speaking. "Peace and blessings."

"Peace and blessings." Was that his own voice?

She was taking the baby home, she said. She lived in a nearby house...She would come again...She hoped he would visit them..."Peace," she said, and she left.

Words had deserted him, but his lips smiled. Peace and blessings, he thought, I know the meaning of peace, I know the meaning of blessing. Nothing he'd ever experienced matched this ecstatic state. He sat motionless, wanting to stay in it for ever.

* * * * *

As the days passed, the ecstasy faded slowly, leaving Naftali in a state of pleasant contentment. Thoughts of home, even of Tamar, receded imperceptibly, leaving him calmer. His sister seemed far off, and he was happy to leave her there, and enjoy his stay in Egypt. He felt he could settle here, just filling the hot uneventful days with little tasks for the family, and being with Michal.

Each morning, before Michal baked bread, Naftali ground the grain in the mill with its two flat stones. He enjoyed watching her make the dough, her hands strong and capable as she mixed coarse meal with water and salt, shaped the loaves, and set them to rise. When Esther was ready to cook, he was there in the courtyard helping to light the fire. When she needed to lift the heavy pot, he was there. Did Michal want to go to the market? Naftali went with her. He was her eyes. He took her hand to guide her along the path, he carried the heavy baskets; a simple peaceful life.

"These beans are greener, take these, Michal. These peppers are juicier, feel them Michal. Here, take this fruit, I bought it for you. Feel how firm the skin. Eat it now, don't wait. There is a bird with blue and yellow feathers, so beautiful…It's flying off now, can you hear it? When it flies, it streaks the sky with bright yellow. A yellow bird in a blue sky."

"What is yellow, Naftali?"

"Yellow is… the sun is yellow. Yellow is the spice Esther puts in the pot with the eggs. They come out yellow. Yellow is the colour of your new dress for the Sabbath, Michal."

"I have no new dress for the Sabbath."

"I want you to have one. I still have money; I'll buy cloth, take it to the dyer, and he'll dye it yellow, to set off your copper colour hair. You'll be like the sun."

She laughed. "What would an old dried-up virgin do with a yellow robe? Better give the cloth to Mariam, to make clothes for Yeshua. That child is growing so fast."

"Michal, do you feel he's a special child?"

She hesitated, "I've never told anyone this before, but something wonderful happens when I hold Yeshua."

"What do you mean?"

"It's almost as if I can see! Not as you see; not things on the outside, but I can see a beautiful light shining right inside myself." The plain features softened, "Can you understand this, Naftali? It really happens."

"I believe you, Michal, I do understand. Do you remember that first day I came to the village? I held Yeshua, and I too received indescribable blessings. There are no words I can use to tell you how wonderful it was, but just thinking of it brings peace."

"Perhaps it's how I feel when I see that light. It's linked with the child, but in a way I don't understand. The child brings blessings. He *is* a special child. Tell me, Naftali, does Yeshua appear different from other children?

"He looks like any other healthy baby, though sometimes he appears to dream, a look comes into his eyes as if he sees things others can't see. I know it sounds fanciful, but lately I've been thinking that he could be the King of the Jews that Herod tried to destroy."

"The son of a carpenter a king? I can't believe that."

"King David was a shepherd boy before becoming a king."

"Will you tell me about him?"

"Tonight, when you're spinning, I'll tell you the story."

But she wasn't to hear it.

That evening at sunset, Naftali climbed to the roof of the house. A huge red sun sank majestically, crimsoning a palm patterned sky. He closed his eyes, lifting his face to the gentle caress of the breeze, grateful for its cooling touch.

Gidean came calling his name. "There is a man outside, he says he's come with a message for you."

Naftali jumped up, and hurried down the steps to be met by his father's servant, Noam, who stood there, ill at ease.

"Noam, can it really be you? Blessed be he who comes. Are you bringing me news from home?"

"I'm happy to have found you, Master Naftali."

"Did my father send you? Come in, I'll bring water, then you can tell me why you've come."

A thousand fears raced through Naftali's mind, but he forced himself to wait courteously while Esther brought water for Noam, who drank slowly. At last he wiped his beard on the back of his hand, looking at Esther, Gidean, and Michal in turn.

"These people are my friends, Noam, they've cared for me well, and I trust them. You can speak."

"Your father sends greetings. He wants you to return immediately. There is a caravan leaving tomorrow morning, and if we go now, we can join it."

"So soon? What's the hurry, is someone ill? Is it my father? What has happened Noam? Have you brought a letter?"

Noam handed him a scroll.

Sivan.

Naftali, Greetings,

Noam has been sent to bring you home. Come as quickly as you can; although I fear it may be too late.

Your sister Tamar is with child. We have questioned her, and she swears Ephraim is not the father. Indeed, he could not possibly be, as they have never been alone together.

Ephraim has not been told. We've only told him Tamar is ill, and can't see him. Soon she will no longer be able to hide herself, and Ephraim will be questioned. When he has sworn he has never lain with her, his family will surely take the matter to the Sanhedrin, alleging adultery. Naturally we greatly fear the consequences.

Hurry home, that you may be of help to us in this difficult time.
Your father, Amos.

Naftali got to his feet, stupefied. There is trouble at home, I must leave immediately."

"You'll come again, Naftali," Michal said, turning away so he could not see her pain.

"Yes, come again," Esther urged," and you will be so welcome."

* * * * *

The journey was interminable. In his impatience to be home, Naftali seethed at delays, begrudging every minute it took to water the animals, and to eat. He felt no need of food, it was like sand in his mouth, and he ate only to sustain life. The desert was hateful, the rocks baleful. By day, his enemy the sun scorched his body, by night the uncaring moon lit the cruel stones. Pick them up, one by one, throw them far away. No stone must touch her; no stone come near the flesh of my sister. Unbearable, the slowness of the journey. What was she doing now? How must she be feeling? A doe with an unborn fawn, defenceless, and the hunters closing in.

At last they reached the sea, its dazzling diamonds hard and unfeeling. Where was peace now? Where was blessing? He could almost laugh to think how carefree he'd felt in Egypt. What was Michal to him now? At one time he's even thought of asking her father for her hand in marriage. Laughable. A wild scheme excited his mind. He would escape with Tamar to Egypt. Here they could live as man and wife, as many an Egyptian brother and sister did, and none would point a finger. They'd live as Egyptians, outside the law of the Hebrews. He would be a Jew exiled from the Jews, but united with Tamar. They would leave Judaea swiftly, and their going would doubtless reveal their secret; incest, an abomination, punishable by death by fire.

He reached his home gaunt and weary, burned by sun and wind, and no gladness of home-coming awaited him. His father met him at the doorway the anxiety in his face confirming Naftali's fears.

"Father, what of Tamar?"

"Ephraim's family found out. Ephraim swore the child was his, although they have never been alone together."

"So they will be wed?"

Amos shook his head sadly, unable to speak, choking back tears. Eventually he whispered, "Tamar was questioned separately by a delegation from the Sanhedrin. She did not know what Ephraim had told them, and she admitted she had never lain with Ephraim. She wouldn't reveal the father." Amos tightened his lips and gripped Naftali by the shoulders. "If I knew who it was, I would hand him straight to the Sanhedrin myself," he said. "He deserves to die. Why should she die alone?"

"Die?"

"The Sanhedrin ruled it." Amos covered his face with his hands, while Naftali waited, cold with dread. "A knowing betrayal of vows taken at the betrothal ceremony is considered to be the same as adultery, punishable by death. It's to be on the fifth day. My own daughter, my little Tamar, for adultery, and the child in her womb." Amos broke down, covering his face with his hands, while Naftali, shocked and numb, waited long moments for him to go on. His father raised teary eyes, "Rachel is sick with grief, and lies on her bed all day. She can't help. So now there is only you to help your sister. Perhaps if you'd been here, this might not have happened. You took no part in the betrothal, running off to Egypt on Temple business when Joseph should have gone himself, then staying away as if the family meant nothing to you. Don't stand there looking so dumb Naftali; go to Tamar. Tell her you'll help her, that you'll stop at nothing. After you've spoken to her, go to Joseph. He said he would do all he could to help, although he was useless in the Sanhedrin. But he has friends amongst the Romans. Something has to done, and fast. Go." He spun Naftali round, pushing him in the direction of Tamar's room.

Chapter Eighteen

The Cave

Rachamim walked beside the creaking cart, stubbing his toes on stones, oblivious to the pain in his bleeding feet. He had eyes only for Menachem. As the wooden wheels jolted over rough ground, he clung to the cart, trying to stop it shaking the frail body inside. Menachem's face was sunken and grey, his eyes closed. Rachamim couldn't tell if he was conscious, only a barely perceptible breath showing him the older man still clung to life. The sun beat down mercilessly as the straining donkey, dark with perspiration, struggled bravely homewards. Amnon guided it grimly, never stopping to drink, but tilting his water-skin as he went, slopping water into his mouth and over his robe, where it dried almost immediately. Rachamim moistened a cloth from his own water-skin, and held it to Menachem's lips, praying silently, begging the Angel of Compassion to let the sufferer reach Qumran before he died.

"Turn here," he said, in a hoarse whisper. Amnon obediently turned the donkey's head, and Rachamim almost sobbed with relief. Qumran at last! If only he could go in.

"You must take him in alone," he said to Amnon.

"Aren't you coming too?"

"No; I may not."

"I don't understand."

"One day I will explain. Now there's no time to talk. Go now quickly." He took a one last look at the beloved face, "Go in peace," he said sadly, stifling a howl of despair, as he broke away, and stumbled towards the cliffs.

Slipping and sliding on the steep path, he struggled up the rock-strewn cliff-face, entered a large dark cave, and collapsed on the ground. At least I have shelter from the heat, he comforted himself. The darkness felt cool on his sunburned skin. He picked up the water-skin, and the last drops of stale water trickled tepid into his mouth. Pushing the useless skin aside, Rachamim closed his eyes.

* * * * *

"I think I'll ask Nissim to take me back home." Yedidyah said.

"You've only been here three days. It's a miracle you're here at all, after the scene your father made over Menachem lending the donkey to help that bad man escape. I never thought he'd let you

111

come. Now you want to go home! Don't you like it here?" Ezra asked.

"It's not how I thought it would be."

"How did you think it would be?"

"I thought I'd spend more time with you and Nissim. Rachamim and Menachem aren't even here, so how can I ever learn to heal?"

"You've got to study first, before you are allowed to learn healing. I'm eleven now, nearly a man, but I had to learn to read and write first, just like you. Afterwards they decide if you can study something else, like healing or astrology, or being a scribe."

"I'd never want to be a scribe. They write all day. Or a teacher. My own teacher is so strict, I can't do anything right. I just laughed this morning, he looked so comical with that fly buzzing round his nose, and he gave me a long talking-to about not laughing. At home I could go out on the hills with Ruhama and Shoshana, and we could laugh all we wanted. Here it's 'Yedidyah, go and bathe, sit quietly, read this, write that,' all day. What do I have to wash so much for? I already bathed at Passover. But yesterday they made me bathe, and today Dinah made me bathe again. Wash, wash, wash! How much washing do I have to do? Then there's the prayers. I'm tired of them already, and I'm sure the Lord is too, hearing the same old words, day after day."

"Well, I'm not bored, and be careful when you talk of the Lord. He's above all feelings."

Yedidyah ignored him. "Did you like being here when you first came?

"I did find it strange at first, although I was born into a family of Essenes, and I'm used to the customs. Now I love it here."

"Even the prayers?"

"Especially the prayers. I feel I can forget myself when I pray."

"But I don't want to forget myself. Why would I want to do that? It's too hot here. Can we go down to the sea and bathe?"

"I thought you didn't like bathing. Maybe one day we can go. Do you want to come with me, and we'll see the goats?"

"I miss Sheleg."

"He wouldn't have been happy here; it's far too hot for him."

"Too hot for me too. Sheleg is much nicer than a whole herd of stinking goats."

"They don't stink, Yedidyah. If you don't want to come, I won't bother. I'll go and see if Nissim needs some help in the herb garden."

"No, let's go and see the goats being taken to graze."

He felt a little freer, walking with Ezra and the goats in the hot afternoon, his new yellow tunic still clean, his freshly-washed hair glinting in the sun. He didn't have to wrap his head in a cloth now, it was growing back nicely, and his mother had trimmed it so it was even. His mother hadn't wanted him to come. She'd been almost glad when Avinoam had shouted at Menachem, calling him a false friend. But Menachem had talked to Avinoam at length, and his father had finally calmed down and admitted it would be a good thing for his son to learn to read, write, and figure. In Qumran, he'd be well taught, and safe. The Qumran school might be a safe place, thought Yedidyah, but it was tiresome. Tonight he was going to have to practise chanting yet again, torturing the one poor note until it came out right. He could have been at home running in the hills, enjoying the breeze, playing with Sheleg. Even the village lads, and that silly Jonathan would have been more fun than the other pupils he'd met here. They spoke with strange accents, and he hadn't made any friends yet, although a boy called Hillel had smiled at him. It was the first time Yedidyah had seen a boy with a black skin, and he found it amusing. Hillel's got hair like a sheep, he mused fondly.

"What's in that cave?" he asked Ezra, pointing to a shadowy entrance in the cliff face.

"Bats, probably. We never go in there."

"I've never seen a bat. What does it look like?"

"It's like a mouse that flies. It's awful."

"I don't think that's awful. I think its interesting. And I'd like to see one."

"Well, you will. They come out at night. They circle around when it's nearly dark."

"Shall we go and find them before they come out? The cave looks exciting, and I think I can climb there easily. Come on Ezra, let's go and explore."

"It's not allowed."

"Who said?"

"Nissim."

"He's not here to see us Ezra, so let's go."

"Listen, Yedidyah, I've still got to do what I'm told, even if no one sees."

"Do you always do what they tell you?"

"I try to. I'd like to be a member of the Brotherhood when I grow up."

"Like Rachamim?"

Ezra nodded. He seemed a little sad at the mention of Rachamim, and Yedidyah wanted to ask him the reason, but his attention was distracted by a goat. She was standing on three legs, scratching an ear. A pretty animal. Perhaps she could be his special pet.

Walking to the school, he made up his mind to go and explore the cave, and see the bats close up. It was something to look forward to during the endless chanting. He studied the cliff side. There didn't appear to be a track leading to the cave, but he was sure he could easily make his own track, providing there was a good moon.

Yedidyah knew better than to tell Ezra of his plan. Ezra was still looking sad. It seemed it had something to do with the reason Rachamim was not in Qumran, but no one would explain anything. Yedidyah had tried to remind Ezra of the baby Immanuel and the beautiful mother, but even this didn't seem to make Ezra happy. It was as if a cloud had come down over the boy's usual cheerfulness. Yedidyah knew all about clouds, but he also knew how to disperse them. He'd learnt how that special night. He had only to think of Immanuel, and he felt better, often recapturing his initial feeling of wonder and delight. It was like magic. Somehow, the image of the infant had merged with the image of Eli, and Immanuel had become Yedidyah's age, his beloved companion, his own little God.

He was chatting to Immanuel in his mind that night as cautiously he emerged from the stifling house, intent on his excursion to the cliffs. But Dinah heard him. "Where are you going, Yedidyah?"

"To see if there's a full moon," he answered truthfully.

"The moon isn't full, but it's a bright one. As it's been so hot, perhaps you'd like to sleep on the roof tonight? You'll be cooler there. Shall I bring up your sleeping mat?"

"I can do it myself, thank you Dinah," Yedidyah said happily. Escape would be simple from the roof.

He had almost reached the mouth of the cave, when he heard the scrunch of footsteps far below. Grabbing the hand of the invisible Immanuel, he crouched behind a rock. Peering downwards, he made out two figures in white, moving slowly as they approached the foot of the cliff, carrying something between them. Yedidyah watched them climb, and as they came nearer, he could see they were carrying a very large clay jar, of the kind used in the Scriptorium to store finished scrolls. Surely they weren't going to put it in his cave? He held his breath as the two paused outside the entrance. He must keep very still, as the slightest movement could dislodge stones and send them rattling down the cliff. The men carefully set the jar near the entrance, and one kindled a small oil lamp. Now he could see them clearly, bearded scribes, still panting with exertion. He could smell the clean scent of their sweat. One of them went into the cave, then called out to his Brother in surprise. What he said brought Yedidyah rushing from his hiding place, and into the cave to see for himself.

The scribes were bending over the body of a man in white who lay unmoving. Disregarding the Brothers' astonished exclamations, Yedidyah edged forward. It was Rachamim who was lying there! Yedidyah began patting his face, urging him to wake.

Someone was calling his name. He could hear it from far away. "Rachamim, Rachamim." He needed to open his eyes, but there was a heavy weight on them. It was better to sink back into oblivion; there was no thirst there. There was a pressure on his lips, and a wetness. No, it couldn't be, he must be dreaming. The water-skin was empty, his legs too weak to take him to fetch water. His parched throat contracted, and his eyes flew open a brief second. Ah, this must be it. I died, and this is the Angel to welcome me to Heaven.

And then he was running. Running through fields of yellow chrysanthemums, holding her hand. She was running with him, blue skirt bright against the yellow. She was singing, his name, Rachamim, Rachamim, and the angels were chanting a well-known hymn, and somehow his lips moved, joining in.

"Thou hast placed me beside a fountain of streams
   in an arid land,
   and close to a spring of waters
   in a dry land
   and beside a watered garden in a wilderness."

And all the while the angels were ministering to him, and he slept holding a hand.

So much light. Where was he? Ah, yes, I'm dead, he remembered, opening his eyes.

"He's awake," Nissim's face swam over him. Nissim must be dead too! Rachamim opened his mouth to speak.

"Don't try to speak yet, Rachamim," Nissim said. "Just rest. You are safe now; you are home."

The angel was sitting beside him, holding his hand. A boy angel, with a shining halo, and blue eyes. He looked familiar.

115

"I'm glad you're better," the angel was saying. "I gave you water in the cave. I'm living here now. Don't you recognise me? It's Yedi-dyah."

Wanting to answer…not finding words…Nissim's loving gaze. Rachamim shut his eyes.

"I'll come back to see you," Yedidyah promised, loosing his hand.

Someone had darkened the cubicle in which he now lay, hanging a heavy cloth over the window. He became aware of a cooling breeze, and turned his head painfully towards it. An attendant Brother was fanning the air with a fan of palm leaves—for him! A single thought rushed through his mind, 'I'm not worthy' and he struggled to speak.

"Don't you know you have to rest quietly, and gather your strength?" Nissim said firmly. "Now it's your turn to learn how to be a patient. Learn it well."

Rachamim lay still, while buzzing clouds of unworthiness fanned round his head like gnats in a summer breeze. But at least he was home. When they found out about the broken vow, he'd be asked to go, but meanwhile he gave himself up to the capable ministration of a Brother sent to tend him. There were cooling drinks, and applications of the pulp of fruits to soothe his torn and bloody feet. And he could hear the chanting. I didn't die, he thought, but this is Heaven, here on earth. If only he could stay.

His strong young body responded quickly to the cure, and on the third day, the Guardian himself came, his vital presence filling the tiny room. He dismissed the attendant with a slight gesture of the right hand, and Rachamim was alone with him. Rachamim had never seen the Guardian at close quarters before, and tried to get up, but the Guardian motioned him to stay lying down.

"When the ten days of your penance were over, and you didn't return, we sent two Brothers to look for you. It wasn't until the fifteenth day that you were found by the scribes, as you know. Now that you are healed, is there anything you would like to tell me before the Community allows you to take your place here again, Brother Rachamim?"

"I broke my vow. I took bread from a stranger."

"How many times?"

"Just the one time. I wanted to be strong to help Menachem."
"Did you succeed in helping him?"

"I failed. The bread couldn't give me the strength to heal."

There was a silence that seemed to last an eternity, but at last the Guardian spoke. "The vow that is broken to save a life can become a blessing. It's like a hand stretched out to pull a man to safety from a pit; permissible even on the holy Sabbath."

Love and relief struggled with sorrow as Rachamim thought of Menachem. "I failed to save a life," he said.

"You seem to have forgotten, Brother Rachamim, that everything is ordained by the Most High. He alone is the author of our going out and coming in. Nothing happens that is not His will. We receive no other than our just deserts at all times."

"I had forgotten," Rachamim said in shame.

"You thought you could do something in your own strength, and that was your sin. How can a mere man heal another alone? Our destiny has been shaped from the beginning of time. You can never be a Inner Initiate of the Qumran Brotherhood, Rachamim." The Guardian paused, and fixed Rachamim with his deep-set eyes. "You can't struggle with your nature," he said.

Uncomprehending, Rachamim waited for him to continue.

"You have not the nature of a celibate, Brother Rachamim," the Guardian explained. "For now, you may stay near Qumran, and join us for work and prayer. When you are twenty, marry, and live outside the Community as a married member."

The Guardian moved to the window and pulled down the dark curtain, which crumpled to the floor. Sunshine flooded in.

"We will send scribes to Jericho to bring you a bride. She will be your betrothed, but you will live apart from her except for the days needed for her to prove herself fit to be a mother. If she is able to bring you strong children, you may marry her, and together you will add to the lustre of the Sons of Light."

When the Guardian had gone, Rachamim wept for the collapse of his dream. He would never take part in the Council of the Pure, never know the joy of initiation into the sacrament of the Meal of the Pure. But he could still work in Qumran, he consoled himself, he was to have a wife, he would be blessed with sons. Words of praise for the goodness of the Nameless One and His Angel of Compassion tumbled disjointedly from his lips. He was to stay near Qumran. Slowly, the tumult of his emotions merged into the deep peace of meditation, and a beautiful face swam before him. Laughing eyes, unbound hair, a crown of yellow flowers, such a smile. Then the vision faded. "Come on, Rachamim, time to go outside."

He opened his eyes reluctantly, and blinked. They were all smiling. Nissim with his unruly curls, Ezra's sharp fox-like face split by a welcome grin, and the beaming features of Yedidyah, the potter's wayward child.

Nissim held a folded robe. "We've come to take you to the mikvah," he said, "you are to bathe and ask forgiveness for your sin."

Yedidyah slipped a strong warm hand in Rachamim's.

"Slowly, Yedidyah," Nissim warned, "He's been ill, we'll go quietly."

As he emerged, newly clean from the purifying waters Rachamim sensed the welcome in the eyes of the Brothers gathered round.

"The priests are waiting to bless you."

Walking in a dream of happiness, Rachamim was ushered into the sacred hall, where he took his place before the priests. As they intoned the blessings, Rachamim ventured one quick glance around the room. At the head of the assembly, next to the Guardian himself, Menachem's face smiled at him in loving recognition.

Chapter Nineteen

Tamar

There was an unfamiliar servant sitting in front of Tamar's room, who sprang to his feet as Naftali rushed towards it.

"Who are you?" he challenged, barring the door.

"What are you doing here?" Naftali growled. "Get out of my way."

The man stood his ground, raising the heavy stick with which he was armed. "I'm here to guard the prisoner, by the order of the family of Manasseh. None goes in without permission."

"And I am here to see my sister. Now will you let me pass?"

"How do I know you are who you say you are?"

"Noam." Naftali shouted.

Noam, still dishevelled from the journey, came out of his quarters. "Tell this person who I am."

"He is Naftali, son of Amos; the son of the house."

The servant reluctantly lowered his stick and stood aside. "Go in," he said grudgingly.

Naftali brushed past into the room. It was unnaturally dark. Thick curtains draped the windows, and the door to the garden was closed. By the light of guttering oil lamps, he made out a strange woman who raised her head suspiciously when he entered. Then Abishag was upon him, clutching him round the knees, whimpering and babbling.

He raised her to her feet. "I'm here now Abishag, it's all right. Where's Tamar? Can you get rid of this woman, whoever she is? Get rid of her. I want to speak with Tamar. Where is she?"

She raised a tear streaked face. "She's sleeping."

Crossing to the little bed, he knelt beside it. A single oil lamp lit her still features. She smelled sour, unwashed hair scattered over the pillow, a cat curled at her feet.

"Oh, my love, Tamar." He picked up a hand, cradling it to his cheek, but Tamar didn't stir, her hand icy in his. "Tamar, my love, Tamar." Still she didn't respond, only the slight rise and fall of the coverlet showing she breathed.

"Abishag," he called urgently. She came, biting at her knuckles, trying not to cry.

"How long has she been sleeping? It's past noon"

"Since yesterday. I don't know. Many hours."

119

"Is she ill? I can't wake her." He tapped Tamar's face. Straightening, he gripped Abishag by the shoulders, shaking the wispy child urgently. "Tell me what has happened to her," he demanded.

"It's the powder Rachel gives her to make her sleep," Abishag whimpered, looking sideways at the servant woman. Naftali dragged the child to the other side of the room, out of earshot, and hissed, "What powder?"

"Rachel makes me give it to Tamar."

"Did Tamar know what it was?"

"Rachel said not to tell her. She said it was kinder."

The servant moved nearer to listen, but Naftali glared at her with such a menacing expression that she backed away, and crouched on her mat in the corner, still watching him. He turned from her, controlling surging emotions with difficulty. "Abishag, I want you to tell me all you know. From the beginning. And don't hide anything, because I'll find out. You trust me, don't you?"

She nodded, dumbly. "Rachel gave me packets of powder. Like this." She held up five fingers. "Every day I have to put one in Tamar's drink; and then, on the fifth day…" her face crumpled.

"Abishag, what have you done? How many powders did you give her? What do you mean, the fifth day?"

"Mistress Rachel said that on the fifth day…" she broke down, crying into her raised hands.

Naftali took her wrists, bringing her hands down. "By the fifth day, what, Abishag?"

"She said that on the fifth day, Tamar would not wake up again. Not ever."

He released her in horror. "Faithless girl! Do you understand nothing? Where are the powders, Abishag? Bring them to me at once."

There were three. Two small packets, and a larger one. "You will not give Tamar any more, even if Rachel asks. Do you understand?" As Abishag nodded, his face softened. Such a little girl, how could she know what Rachel intended, how could she know what to do, whom to obey? "We are going to cheat the Sanhedrin, Abishag," he whispered, "You must believe me." A flicker of hope crossed the little face.

"Will you help?"

"I'd do anything. I'll die in her place." Her voice rose.

"Be quiet. Do you want her to hear?" he indicated the watching servant. "Nobody's going to die, but you must do as I say." He turned to go. "I'll come back as soon as I can, and while I'm gone please take proper care of your mistress. Open the windows, let some light in here, and then try to wake her. When she's awake, take her to bathe, and help her stay awake. Do your best, and be assured it will go well."

She seemed to have understood, and Naftali went out quickly to where his father was waiting in the outer courtyard.

"You saw Tamar?"

"She's sleeping. Tell me father, are those servants always there guarding her? Do they ever go away? What about at night?"

"They are always there during the day; and others come to take their place at night. All paid by the family of Ephraim ben Manasseh, her betrothed," his lip curled, "with the full sanction of the Sanhedrin, of course," he added bitterly.

"Father, try not to despair. I've thought of a way. Joseph will help us. I'm going there now."

* * * * *

The friends embraced wordlessly. Then taking Naftali's hand, Joseph said quietly, "Come, we'll talk."

He lead him to a small side room, calling to the servant to bring wine and see they were not disturbed.

"I've already tried everything I could in the Sanhedrin," Joseph began, "but without any success."

"So we try the Romans?"

"I've already tried. The Procurator gave me the usual reasons. 'Romans don't interfere with Jewish jurisdiction in the case of punishments for citizens.'...As I expected."

"Then we'll have to get her out ourselves."

"I noticed she's guarded by servants. I went yesterday."

"Did you speak to Tamar?"

"She was sleeping. I thought it kinder not to rouse her rouse her. Her mother gave her sleeping powders...Rachel's way of cheating the executioners!" Naftali pulled the packets from his girdle and eyed them thoughtfully. "I'm thinking they can be very useful."

"We give them to the servants?"

"Exactly. And then we smuggle Tamar out. But where can she go? Where can we possibly hide her? Jerusalem's full of Sanhedrin members. They'll alert the Romans, who are bound to uphold so-called Jewish justice. She'll have to go to another town; maybe a village somewhere."

Joseph looked at him gravely. "Do you think I haven't thought of that? But the Law extends even outside Judaea. Galilee is so well patrolled now because of all the trouble with the Zealots, and Idumaea and Samaria are almost as bad. She can't stay in this country."

"Shall we take her to Egypt?"

"I've thought of that. I even made inquiries. The next caravan for Egypt, the only one I can trust, doesn't leave for three weeks. And at this busy time of the year, I doubt we'll get a passage from Jaffa to Alexandria either."

"India then?"

"You know better than that. The laws in India are equally harsh. An unmarried mother with a child? Impossible!"

"Then where, Joseph? What shall we do?"

"You remember Pallas, my Greek concubine?"

"Of course. How could I forget? But what has this to do with Tamar?"

"Everything. Tamar needs to go where she will be cared for and welcomed, and Pallas is just the woman to help her. She has a large, comfortable house which I rent for her and our child, and Tamar could go to live with her. The Greeks are liberal, and Tamar can stay there undisturbed. Once she's settled, you'll be able to visit her. What do you say?"

"It sounds a wonderful plan Joseph my friend; I knew I could count on you. But how can we possibly get her to Greece? And without anyone suspecting it's you who've helped us? No one in the Sanhedrin is stupid; they all know about the close ties between us, and they'll be watching you. If this comes out, you lose your place there, and risk imprisonment and ruin. Then what about Sarah and the twins? How can I let you do this?"

"I can't imagine how you can refuse. Tradespeople come and go here all day, and it's possible some may be spies for the Sanhedrin. So I'm going to talk very quickly, and tell you my plan. Listen and tell me what you think. When the servants are asleep we take Tamar and Abishag out of the house. I'll have a consignment of wool packed and ready in the covered wagon. The women can travel with it, and I'll ride alongside. We'll go straight to Jaffa, where, for a certain sum, I know I can get places on a sailing vessel for my two cousins, Tamar and Abishag. If there's space for one more passenger, I'll go along with them, but if..." He broke off anxiously. Someone was at the door.

But it was Sarah, her face blotchy with weeping. She greeted Naftali coldly, averting her eyes. She's guessed, and she blames me for Tamar's predicament, Naftali thought, hating himself.

"Shall I send for food, Joseph?" Sarah asked.

"Later, Sarah, later. We're planning something," he whispered.

"Ah!" She brightened. "How can I help?"

"I don't think you can, Sarah."

"I'll do anything…" Her lip trembled, and she pulled her veil over her face, hiding her tears.

Joseph stared at her reflectively. "Perfect," he said. "Do you see that Naftali?" He turned to Sarah. "You may be able to help us after all, my dear. You and Tamar are the same height." He leaned forward in his chair, and beckoned Sarah close. "Tomorrow, early in the morning, you and Devorah visit Tamar. Take the twins. The guards will be sound asleep. Naftali you'll have to see to that. Sarah, you and Devorah change clothes with Tamar and Abishag. Devorah is much fatter than Abishag, but luckily no taller. You'll think of something no doubt. It's important that you wear your usual dress, Sarah, so people recognise it's you going in, and use a thick veil to cover your face. Tamar and Abishag can walk out carrying the babies, I'll meet them in the courtyard, and bring them home. Where else would a father bring his wife and children? As soon as you and Devorah return to look after the twins, I start for Jaffa."

"I'll do it of course, Joseph, but I won't wear Tamar's dress. What if I'm seen in it on the way home? It would be obvious who had helped Tamar. And Devorah certainly can't pass for Abishag. What if Devorah were to stay at home with the twins, and let her little Huldah come with me? She and Abishag are very alike, and who notices what a servant is wearing? But how are the two of us to get home?"

"There's a door hidden in the wall of the courtyard, behind the yellow creeper," said Naftali. Tonight I'll take a stout knife to cut the creeper, and force the door open if I can."

"And if you can't, and we are seen?"

"Our family will be known accomplices in Tamar's escape," said Joseph calmly.

"Never!" said Naftali, "I'll get that door open if I have to break it down." He hugged Joseph, "It's a wonderful plan. How can we thank you, both of you?"

"By playing your part well. Make sure those servants sleep soundly. We don't want to kill them, but they do need a strong dose."

"I'll see to it now."

"Go in peace."

* * * * *

Naftali raced through hot dusty alleyways, making for the market. He pressed through a knot of women at the basket-maker's stall,

"I'll take this one."

The stall keeper named a huge sum, looking at Naftali in amazement as the shekels were pushed into his palm. Seizing the basket, Naftali stuffed it full of provisions and rushed homewards, oblivious of everything but one thought; Tamar must be saved.

Pausing just long enough to reassure his father, he was rewarded by a tremulous smile before he plunged into the kitchen and confronted the cook. She was sitting by the cooking pot, stirring half-heartedly. She looked up red-eyed as he came in.

"What are you cooking?"

"A stew of vegetables only. No one wants to eat."

"Well, put in good things." He emptied the basket of its contents. "Put herbs, bake fresh bread. What is all this stale stuff?" He pointed to a shelf where dried-out bread lay dusty and unprotected from flies. "Tonight we feast," he said firmly. "It's a farewell to Tamar."

Her raised hands failed to smother her shriek of dismay.

"No, Abigail, not the stones! Freedom! Tamar will be taken to safety tomorrow, the Lord willing. Now will you make her some good food?"

Crying with relief, she got up, noticing as if for the first time the disarray in the kitchen.

"There's one more thing, Abigail, before you start." Swiftly he outlined his plan for drugging the servants.

"I'll take care of it, Master Naftali, have no fear. Yael has nimble fingers. When the cook from the Manasseh family comes bringing food for their servants, Yael will meet her and offer to carry it. She can slip in the powders on the way. Yael," she shouted, "where are you? Where are you hiding? Come quickly."

With Yael scampering in his wake, Naftali hurried to Rachel's room, and knocked loudly at the door. No answer. He knocked again, but it was his father who opened the door a crack.

"I must speak to Rachel."

Amos said sadly, "Rachel is mourning Tamar as if she's already dead. I've tried to reassure her, but she doesn't seem to understand, or respond. The shock has been too great. She's complaining of terrible pains in the head; she can't talk to you or anyone now."

"I understand. I'll speak to her when she feels better." Now there was no way to find out the strength of the powders, but he couldn't afford to delay. He turned to Yael. "Take these." Digging in his girdle, he pulled out the three packets. And may it not kill them, he prayed inwardly, noticing his hands. The hands of a murderer? Certainly they were very dirty. He was still wearing a travel-stained robe, his hair hanging tangled and dusty.

In his room, he pulled fresh garments from a chest, and taking soaps and perfumed oil, went to bathe.

There was a different servant outside Tamar's door, and again Naftali was forced to identify himself. He could hear laughter coming from the room.

Tamar was playing with the cat. She straightened as he came in, dropping her arms to her side, head proudly erect. Her belly swelled under a faded dress, loose hair tumbled round her pallid face.

Tamar spoke first. "Peace Naftali, blessed be he who comes." Compassion, love, guilt and pain washed over him. All he could say was her name, "Tamar."

She turned to the watching woman, "Leave us."

The servant shrugged, and went out to the terrace, leaving the door ajar.

Tamar came and slipped her hand into Naftali's. "I knew you'd come, even before Abishag told me you were here."

He wanted to kneel before her dignity and courage, he wanted to take her in his arms and comfort her, but instead he stood mute, sick with guilt.

She guided his hand to her belly. "Ours."

"Yes."

"Can you save her?"

"Tomorrow." He bent close to her ear, "There's a plan."

Her eyelids flickered her understanding. "Can I take Abishag? And the cat?"

"I bought a basket." He loosed her hand, breaking away as the door opened, but it was Yael. She came in holding a jar and a basket of food.

"For us?" Tamar asked.

"For the servant woman. Where is she?"

Naftali indicated the garden. "Take it to her," he ordered.

* * * * *

Both servants fell asleep with frightening speed. One sagged open-mouthed outside the door, the other sprawled on her back in the garden. Abishag, worn out by her ordeal, slept too, hugging the cat.

When night had fallen, Naftali carried a blanket into the little lamp-lit courtyard. He dragged the sleeping servant aside, strewed the blanket with cushions, and motioned to Tamar. "Come, Tamar, rest here, and eat," he said, "Abigail has prepared food."

"I'll eat later. There's so much I want to tell you." She sat down facing him. "You were not there when I found I was with child, and I didn't know who to tell. It was terrible, being so alone, knowing what would happen if it was discovered. Better to kill the baby myself I thought, than have it die inside me in the grave. So I went to Mother, and she gave me herbs...to make the baby fall." She couldn't look at him. "Please understand, Naftali, I didn't want to die. I was so afraid … I didn't want to die. But every time I tried to drink the herbs, a violent nausea rose up here," she pointed to her throat, "the mixture spewed from my mouth, and I couldn't swallow. I hated you then, Naftali, I felt you'd killed us both, me and our child."

He waited, dumb with distress, for her to go on.

"Ephraim must be so sad now. When I'm gone, I want you to tell him I'm safe, and I'm so sorry for the pain I caused him."

"I'll tell him."

"You were not here when I needed help, but Ephraim was. He stood by me in the trial, he even said the child was his. How I wish that was true. We might have been happy together," she said wistfully.

"Do you hate me still, Tamar?"

"No, Naftali, I couldn't kill my love for you, just as I couldn't kill our baby. But all the passion died. I think I'll always love you, but it's a different love. It's the love a sister feels for her brother. Ephraim was gentle, he made me laugh, he gave me a cat...but that's all over now."

He couldn't find words to express his regrets. He got up abruptly, and went to the creeper, attacking its branches with his knife, stripping off flowers and leaves, not stopping till he'd uncovered a door. When he was satisfied the door could be opened, and the despoiled foliage kicked away, Naftali stooped and picked up a single flower. "Do you see this flower," he asked thoughtfully, "the Avionah, the flower they call Desire?"

"It's beautiful."

"It flowers only at night. In the morning it will be dead. Desire dies like that too."

"And your desire for me? Is it dead? How do you feel for me, Naftali?"

He sat, pulled Tamar towards him, cradled her head in his lap, stroked her hair with gentle hands. What could he say?

"When I was in Egypt, I held a child. As I held him, I experienced something I had often dreamed of, but never thought I would feel. I wish I could describe it to you, but I haven't the words."

"Will you try?"

"It was a love so pure, so divine, so complete in itself, that it needed no object. Nothing else mattered except to be in that love. There was no desire. Thinking back on it, that day I was freed from wrongful desire. I can love you like a dear sister."

"You say the love you felt was divine, Naftali; but how could love be divine, when our God is a God of revenge and punishment?"

"Perhaps He is not."

"They would have stoned me and the innocent child, by God's will. And had they found out about us, we would both have been burned. Is that not cruelty?"

"But they did not find out, and they won't stone you. Precious dove, you and the child will live. Isn't that God's will too? That you be saved?"

"If all goes well, and we are saved, do you think the Lord willed it?"

"All will go well, my heart's treasure, by His will."

"You said you held a child, Naftali. We have till morning. Will you tell me about him?"

Sitting on the ground with Tamar's head on his lap, Naftali remembered the song Mariam had sung to her child. He sang it to Tamar, who worn out with the terrors she'd endured, soon fell asleep as Naftali waited for the morning.

Chapter Twenty

The Chalice

Lying on his mat in the furnace of the tent, Rachamim assured himself nightly that it was no dream. Shulamith really was in Qumran. Accompanied by the two scribes sent to fetch her from Jericho, she had slipped into the settlement as welcome as morning dew, a bundle of herbs her only dowry. Beautiful Shulamith in her blue dress, beautiful virgin-widow Shulamith, betrothed to him in a simple ceremony. She'd been taken to live with Dinah, until the time she'd be allowed to share his tent. Throughout the long summer days, when fiery air shimmered over the motionless sea, Rachamim would catch glimpses of her as went about her allotted tasks, carrying water to the herb garden. My Shulamith is like a cooling breeze in the scorching air, like a blue petalled flower in the desert, he thought, longing for that brief half hour of the day when they were permitted to talk to each other. He delighted in the sweet amusement in her demurely downcast eyes, in sharing her smiles and modest laughter. How could he wait till he was twenty to marry her? It was an eternity, an eternity! He lived in almost unbearable anticipation of the sacred occasion when they would come together in the bridal tent; for there could be no marriage until Shulamith had proved herself capable of bearing sons.

* * * * *

Reluctantly, Rachamim handed the palm fan to an attendant, and left the House of the Sick for the last time. Two skilled healers had come from Alexandria to stay in the Settlement, and they would work with the sick, freeing Rachamim to do other work. Much against his will. Although the healing energy no longer flowed through his hands, he'd been very happy washing and feeding the patients, and nursing them back to health. Now he was to work in the pottery, a place in which he hadn't the slightest interest.

"Even if the healing energy doesn't flow through me any more, I can still be of use to the sick," he pleaded with Menachem.

The older man looked at him with great tenderness. "It's for your own protection, Rachamim, until you learn to bridle your compassion,"

"How will I know when that has happened, if I no longer work as a healer?"

"You don't have to work with the sick to be a healer," had been the enigmatic answer.

Rachamim went out into the oven-hot night, going over these strange words in his mind, thinking gloomily of the next day. Songs of praise rose peacefully towards a starry sky as he walked slowly to take his place amongst the worshippers. Any movement in this oppressive heat was difficult, and he thought with dread of the next day, when he was to start work in the pottery.

* * * * *

Brothers in dusty work clothes were already toiling to complete the southern wall of the pottery shed when Rachamim arrived early the following morning. Under an awning of coarse cloth offering scant protection from the crippling rays of the sun, Nathan the chief potter greeted Rachamim with enthusiasm.

"Let me show you what we make here." He pointed proudly to neatly ranged utensils of every shape and size, some finished and baked in the kiln, some in the process of drying. Rachamim glanced with indifference at fat round cooking pots, tall storage jars, and sundry other containers.

"And this is how we make the utensils." Nathan said proudly, guiding his new apprentice to a bench where an assistant formed pliable coils, building them up to form a jar.

Perhaps I could get used to doing that, it looks simple enough, Rachamim conceded to himself, watching the assistant incise designs in the clay ... or even that might just be bearable he thought, as Nathan demonstrated the wheel, shaping a graceful pot from a mere lump of clay.

But Nathan picked up a mallet. "You will be preparing the earth for clay making," he said, "I'll show you what to do, and then you'll work at it in both the work periods. At present we need so many large storage jars, that the pottery is now open longer hours. From to-morrow I expect you here one hour earlier in the morning, and the work will continue one hour past the usual finishing time. Don't distress yourself Brother Rachamim," he smiled, "you will still have time for evening prayers."

Squatting, Nathan began to pulverise the hard lumps of earth, muscles bulging in strong arms. "Finish hammering out all the lumps, then pick out any straw and other impurities that remain. I want you to do it very carefully, because if there are any lumps at all, the pots will break. Use the sieve for the finer impurities, and if you have any questions, ask my assistant, as I will be busy with the wheel today."

Bundling his robe up into his girdle, Rachamim picked up the heavy mallet, and pounded. At each blow, dust flew up in a cloud, and within a few minutes, he was coated in it. He toiled on miserably, stopping often to drink from the clay water pitcher. The sweltering morning dragged by, and by the time the signal was given to go to bathe before the meal, Rachamim's head was reeling, his hands swollen and blistered.

Perhaps Nathan will give me other work this evening, he thought, envying the Brother sitting calmly under the awning, rolling long clay coils.

But that evening, his work was the same. And the next day too. Was this interminable task ever going to finish? Nathan's sharp eyes picked out even the tiniest impurities in the clay dust, and Rachamim was asked to sieve it again and again and again. Anger bubbled up in him, and he smashed down hard with the mallet, picking out stones of resentment, straws of jealousy. He should be tending the sick now, that was what he'd been trained for, not this dusty work. The angrier he became, the harder he pounded, and the higher the dust flew. But if Nathan noticed Rachamim's anger, he said nothing, remaining cheerfully engrossed in his own work.

Not even the thought of Shulamith calmed Rachamim's rage. The pottery was situated near a cistern, but it wasn't the one she used to draw water for the garden. He hardly saw her during the day, and the precious time he was allowed to spend with her in the evening was now much shorter because of the longer working hours. Rachamim's prayers were empty of love, his sleep disturbed by the twitching of muscle unaccustomed to so much exertion. The time for the first of the monthly visits to the marital tent was near. He was going to fail her.

He didn't raise his head when he heard light footsteps behind him, and the water caught him by surprise. Trickling over his tangle of dusty curls, it mixed with the clay dust on his tunic, streaking it with mud.

Straightening painfully, Rachamim turned and saw Yedidyah, grinning like a small fiend, shaking the last drops of water from the drinking jar over the carefully sieved pile of earth.

"What are you doing here? You should be studying."

"We finish early in the afternoons now, because of the heat. What are you doing, Brother Rachamim?"

"You should know what I'm doing, you a potter's son! I was preparing earth for clay, until you ruined it for me." He pointed sternly at the damp clods.

Yedidyah started to laugh. "You look so funny! All lined with dirt. Streaks of it down your face."

Rachamim glared, brandishing the mallet.

Yedidyah picked up a sieve. "I'll help. I'm sorry. I just thought I'd cool you down a bit. You looked so hot and cross."

Working with the boy, Rachamim's anger evaporated as quickly as the water from his clothing. It was good to have a helper.

"Look, Rachamim, how fine and pure it is," Yedidyah triumphed, scooping up a handful of dust and sprinkling it back on the pile. "I've collected quite a good heap of stones too."

He's actually enjoying it, Rachamim thought. But he doesn't have a prospective bride to please.

Nathan came out of the pottery shed with a newly fired jar in his hand. Ignoring Yedidyah, he turned to Rachamim, holding up the jar to show the fine lines. "Aren't you pleased with it?"

"It's a fine jar, but I didn't make it."

"Whoever made a jar without clay? Without your work, it could never have been made, so thank you for your help." He looked at Yedidyah sternly. "What are you doing here boy?"

"Rachamim needed cooling," Yedidyah muttered.

"What did you say?"

"I said I'm helping Rachamim."

"Where is your respect for your elders? I don't know how you can be much help."

"My father's a potter."

"And you want to be one too?"

"No, I want to be a healer, like Rachamim, but no one's ready to teach me yet. All I hear is 'wait, and be patient'. I have time, so I came here to ask if I could make something in the pottery. Can I Brother Nathan? I want to make a cup."

"Ask me tomorrow." He hadn't missed the clods of clay, or Rachamim's streaked face. "Boys who pour water over their seniors aren't welcome in the pottery."

"I'm sorry, Rachamim. I won't do it again, I thought you'd enjoy it. So will you let me come, Brother Nathan?"

"We'll see. Ask me tomorrow."

The next day, Yedidyah came again, and the next. It was the same every day.

"Can I make something, Brother Nathan?"

"Ask me tomorrow."

"You said that yesterday."

"Ask me tomorrow, Yedidyah, and be careful how you ask."

"What do you think he means, Rachamim? Isn't he ever going to let me make something? I really want to. He said to be careful how I asked. How can I do that?"

"Try helping me. Help me pick out the stones, and when you've done it a few days, ask again. Anyway, what do you want with a cup?"

"It's for Immanuel. When he comes, I'll be able to give it to him. When he was born, I saw you all giving gifts, beautiful costly ones, and I'd have liked so much to give one too. Only I don't have one. Now it looks as if I won't have one, ever."

"How do you know Immanuel will come here?"

"How did you know Shulamith would come? I just know, that's all."

"Why don't you tell Nathan what you've just told me? Tell him respectfully. That's what he meant when he said be careful how you asked. Maybe he'll listen and let you do it, especially if I put in a good word about my helper," he added.

* * * * *

The permission finally granted, a triumphant Yedidyah wriggled onto the work bench, and started rolling clay.

He came every day. First he helped Rachamim clean the earth, and then worked on the clay. His clever fingers knew how to build up the coils, and at the end of the work period, he'd slide off the bench to show Rachamim his work.

"Look at this one, Rachamim. What do you think?"

"It's beautiful, Yedidyah."

"But not good enough. Tomorrow I'll make another."

Rachamim was growing stronger, his muscles no longer ached, his arm lifting the mallet with ease. But as the heat of the summer increased, so did Rachamim's frustration at the misery of that special night. Every month, she would send word that the time had arrived, she had been through the purification ceremony, she was ready to receive him. And he would go into the furnace of the bridal tent with her, and fail to know union, the heat of his desire for her crippled by fear of losing her to the implacable heat.

"And this one, Brother Rachamim?" Yedidyah's voice interrupted his secret thoughts.

"The best you've made."

"It's still not good enough. Tomorrow."

Every day it was 'tomorrow, tomorrow', until the shelf was full of Yedidyah's yesterdays, and still he wasn't satisfied.

"I can't do it Brother Nathan. It doesn't come as I want it," Yedidyah complained.

"And if I were to help you?"

"It's my gift, so I need to do it alone."

"But I could show you how. Would you like that?"

"I'd like it."

Nathan picked up coiled clay, worked steadily, and a wonderful shape took form under his hands.

"Yes, it's good, even for Immanuel," Yedidyah conceded.

"Will you take it as a model, to copy?"

"No, thank you Nathan, it's got to be my own design. But now I've seen how you work, I think I can improve."

It took six days.

"It's perfect, Yedidyah," Rachamim praised, "an unusual shape, though it looks more like a chalice for a Passover feast than a cup. It's good work."

The boy set it to dry covered with a damp cloth, lest it harden too quickly, and crack.

"We will fire it in the kiln when it's ready," Nathan said. "I'll do it myself. You worked hard, and it's a fine chalice. Come again if you want to make another."

"No, thank you, Brother, I'll never make a cup again. It took too many tries. The Bedouin came with goats, and I'm going first to see them, and after, I'm going to play a game with their children." He skipped off, humming.

* * * * *

If they turn me away, I don't know what I'll do, Amnon thought anxiously, as he came in sight of Qumran. The purification he'd undergone in Jerusalem had not been sufficient; he still felt defiled, a man who had committed abomination. Even here in this holy place he doubted he could atone for his sin, though he knew that penitents had come here before, and found forgiveness. But what if Menachem is dead he asked himself? That too, will have been my fault, not returning the donkey in time, delaying in Jerusalem, seeking vainly for absolution in the Temple. I seem to be good only for causing pain, he mourned.

The watchman at the gate was courteous. "Have you come for healing?"

"I'm not ill, but I'd like to stay a few days, if it's possible. I was here before, when I came to bring Brother Menachem and the donkey." He waited in the vain hope that the watchman would volunteer some information about Menachem.

"How is Brother Menachem" he forced himself to ask, "Did he recover fully?"

"Blessed be the Nameless One, Menachem is well. I remember you bringing him, but you didn't stay long."

"I hurried back to my uncle in Jericho." In fact, he'd rushed off straight away, dreading discovery. Who would want to associate with a defiler of children, a fugitive from the anger of a whole village?

"Wait here," said the watchman, and I'll bring someone to look after you."

"Amnon, welcome." It was Rachamim, a strong bronzed Rachamim, quite unlike the tortured man who'd turned to the cliffs and ran that day. Perhaps Menachem didn't tell him what I did to Yedidyah, Amnon thought. But if Menachem sees me here, he may ask me to go away, push me out.

But Menachem didn't push him out. When he heard Amnon's uncle was dead, he said, "it would be good if you could stay here with us and we'll consider how to go about your healing.

"I'm not sick."

"Your purification then. You'll stay in the House of the Sick, as a working patient, and help with the building work until a course of treatment has been decided for you. I'll show you where to bathe, but you are not free to go anywhere else in the settlement . Food will be sent to you, and if you like, I'll send someone to pray with you. Those are my terms. Do you agree to them?"

Amnon would have agreed to anything. "I agree," he said quickly.

After a simple meal, he stretched out on a mat in the House of the Sick. It was autumn, the month of Tishreh, and the nights were still very hot. He lay listening to the sound of chanting, but it brought him no peace. He missed his father. The villagers would be enjoying cooler weather now, the grapes harvested, and his father alone in the house. I'll go back to the village when I leave here, he decided. Better go back and face my punishment than live so alone, so lonely.

The building work Amnon was given was hard, the stones heavy, and his arms ached. It would be good to rest and drink water. He reached for the jug, but it was nearly empty, and there was no sign of the Brother in charge of the building work. Where was the cistern? Shading his eyes with his hand, Amnon looked over to the southern wall, where he judged the cistern to be. He could see the conduit leading to the water, but Menachem had forbidden him to leave the enclosure. Perhaps if I just look out over the wall, he thought, someone may be there who will fill the jug for me.

Holding the jug, he leaned out over the wall, and started back in guilty surprise. It was the boy! Staring straight at him. Wild-eyed, Yedidyah hurled what he was carrying to the ground, and fled.

Chapter Twenty One

The Day of Atonement

At least the servants hadn't died, Naftali consoled himself, as he waited impatiently for Joseph's return. His agitation grew with the passing of each day and he found himself tracking with increasing frequency to his friend's house, only to be met with Sarah's, 'Not yet! Not yet!' Joseph should have been back long ago, Naftali thought, his mind conjuring dreadful pictures of Tamar and Joseph bleeding and dying by the roadside, while Abishag wandered alone to starve.

Waiting was made even harder by the relentless approach of the dreaded Day of Atonement. Daily the ram's horn blared from the Temple, calling people to prayer and repentance. These were the Days of Awe when the Recording Angel reviewed the sins of every man and woman of Israel. Only those who had confessed and repented would be inscribed in the Book of Life, and Naftali had done neither. He didn't even attempt to pray, considering it worthless without a confession he had no intention of making. Yet without his father's forgiveness, he was doomed to live outside the covenant of Israel, a Godless sinner struck from the Book of Life. His very entrails contracted at the thought.

Amos now spent hours at his wife's side, for Rachel had not recovered from the shock of Tamar's sentencing. Never very stable before, she tossed restlessly on her bed, in a darkened room, and nothing Amos could do was able to calm her. Physicians came and went, but in vain. Their drugs soothed her briefly, but when the effect wore off, she was as frantic as before.

"I want us to go together to the Temple, Naftali," Amos said. "Rachel isn't getting any better, and I fear it's the wrath of the Lord come down on us for refusing to give up our daughter to justice. I've been so preoccupied with Rachel, I haven't yet offered any sacrifice at all, and soon it will be too late. The Day of Atonement will be here, and neither of us has made an atonement offering. We can offer sacrifice, and pray for Rachel and Tamar at the same time. We'll go tomorrow."

The very idea of sacrifice revolted Naftali. Of what good was blood sacrifice without repentance? In his present state, his offering could never help Rachel recover, nor bring blessings on Tamar. Useless to even consider it. But Amos was insistent, and Naftali had reluctantly to agree.

The Outer Court of the Temple was crammed with pilgrims carrying offerings. Money-changers haggled and bargained, exchanging foreign coins for Temple coinage, raucous vendors shouted their wares, animals cried, imprisoned doves beat futile wings. With the din of the crowd oppressing their ears, Naftali and Amos struggled on. Carrying two sacrificial ewe lambs, they pushed through the Court of Women, and into the Court of the Israelites, stopping at a low wall. Here in the shadow of the dazzling white Sanctuary, regal with gold, the priests waited with their long knives.

As Amos presented his offering, Naftali stood clutching his own helpless lamb. Thick clouds of incense mingled with the reek of blood from the steaming altar, sickening him, and he sank his face into the curly pelt.

"What does the Lord want with the blood of beautiful animals?" he mumbled to his astonished father, and dropped the lamb. Leaving the terrified animal to the mercies of the crowd, Naftali staggered through the courtyard retching as his mouth filled with bile.

Lying restless and uneasy on his bed, he heard Amos return. After greeting Noam, his father pushed open Naftali's door and came in. I'll tell him now, Naftali decided swiftly.

Amos said, "I want you to know I am greatly displeased, Naftali. Your behaviour today was totally unacceptable. I thought I should never live to see this sort of disrespect in a son of mine. I need not remind you the Day of Atonement is almost here, and you have yet to offer sacrifice. If you have anything for which you need to atone, do it soon; buy another lamb. Do I have to remind you of the consequences of sins not atoned for?" He turned and went out of the room, too angry to wait for Naftali to reply.

I must go to him and give him a chance to forgive me if he can, Naftali though miserably. The Lord knows I find it impossible to forgive myself! He paced restlessly in the room. Should he speak to his father tonight? How could he add to his father's pain? Better to die himself than cause more suffering.

The time for the evening meal came and went, but the idea of food nauseated him. He lay down on the bed, where his thoughts tortured away all possibility of sleep. Finally, with everyone asleep, Naftali got up, and padded barefoot to the large cupboard outside his father's room. Quietly he opened it. Green glass bottles gleamed in the light of his lamp. Which one would make him sleep, and loosen the knot of fear and despair? He removed a stopper and released a pungent scent. This was no sleeping potion, nor the next, nor the next. Naftali opened bottle after bottle, jar after jar, hands shaking, head reeling, until a single thought hammered in his head. 'Drink this one, do, Naftali, sleep will come. Without atonement, a man is already dead, so drink deep.' The golden liquid glistened seductively. 'Drink deep, drink deep, it will help you forget.' He raised it to his lips. It tasted vile, but he drained it, replacing it carefully on the shelf before lurching to his room. And still sleep didn't come. Instead a cold sweat broke out over his body, making him shiver uncontrollably, huddled wakeful on the bed till morning ... the morning Joseph came.

"Master Naftali," Noam said, " Master Joseph has arrived. He's waiting to see you."

"I am unwell, Noam. Have Master Joseph visit me here." He managed to pull a blanket round himself, before falling back on the bed.

"Joseph, it's been so long. We waited and waited. When will he come, when will he come?"

"I'm here now, Naftali. But what's the matter with you?" He bent to embrace his friend. "You're so cold, are you ill? Have you called the physician. Or shall I get one now?"

"No, don't go, It will pass. I wanted to sleep. I took a strong potion."

He struggled to sit up. "Tell me everything, Joseph. What news of Tamar? I've been sick with fear for her and for your safety. You were gone so long."

"It all went well," Joseph smiled, "there's much to tell you."

"Tell me quickly then. But I'm forgetting. You are tired from the journey, I'll send for refreshment."

"It's you who look as if you need refreshment, my poor Naftali. First be assured all is well with Tamar. The child..."

"Child?" Naftali had almost forgotten the baby. "It was not expected until this month. Is that why you delayed, to wait for the arrival of the child? How is it with the child?"

"The child came early," Joseph frowned, "maybe because of the journey. The road to Joppa was so crowded; pilgrims, soldiers, traders, the whole population seemed to have chosen that day to be on the road. There was also the fear of discovery, especially when I was hailed by Flavius, on his way to the port. He failed to understand why I didn't want to stop at the tavern and drink with him. The ship to Greece was delayed, he said, and was I so changed by my new status in the Sanhedrin that I had no time for an old friend? All this was very frightening for Tamar, hidden as she was in the back of the wagon while I joined Flavius in the inn. How could I refuse? He's been so helpful to us in the past."

"Never mind Flavius. Tell me about the child. When did the child come? Was it during the journey?"

"Be patient, I'll tell you everything. We had already arrived in Greece when the child came. The crossing itself was easy, but then there was the long journey by road to Athens. It was all too much for Tamar. We had been at Pallas' house only one day, when Tamar complained of feeling pains, and the baby was born after a long travail."

"Poor Tamar. But she's well? How is my sister? Joseph, don't hide anything from me. I can see from your face all isn't as it should be." He gripped Joseph's arm anxiously.

"Tamar is well, there is a little daughter."

"A daughter!" Thank the Lord. But it's wonderful! So why are you looking pained? Why didn't you come back sooner? Why did you wait so long? Does that mean the child is not well?"

"The baby was born too soon, Naftali, and she's very small. I waited to see if she would live."

"But she's alive, she'll grow won't she? Isn't she perfect? Has she all her limbs?"

"We waited for the child to respond to us, but she lay always very still, and so we feared she couldn't see."

"How can you know? There's time! Did you ask the physician? She will smile when she sees Tamar's face, when she sees her mother."

"I waited till the physicians could be sure. Naftali, I'm so sorry to be the one to tell you this. She can't see. Your little girl is blind."

Naftali buried his head in his hands. So little, to be in the dark. Always. "Will it be always, Joseph? Can't she be cured?"

"We brought the finest physicians, but there was nothing they could do."

Naftali thought of Michal: 'What is yellow, Naftali?' 'Like the sun' he'd said, 'like the bird, yellow against the sky.' The little one would never see a bird, never see Tamar, never see the sky. It was unbearable. He couldn't even weep, but sat dazed, not moving when Amos came in, and Joseph was forced to repeat the terrible news.

"Tamar has been punished for breaking the law," Amos said sadly, "and her sins have been visited on the child. Forgive me, Joseph, for not staying with you. I am deeply indebted to you, and will speak with you later, but Rachel is very disturbed this morning, and I must get back to her."

"I'm sorry to hear it," Joseph said, "has it been a long time?"

"It started when Tamar became with child. Rachel says unspeakable things … Raves about Naftali and Tamar till I have to beg her to stop."

One quick glance shot between the friends.

"The Essene healers from Qumran are in Jerusalem," Amos went on, "and they've agreed to come here on the Day of Atonement. Everybody will be at prayer, but it seems they have a different calendar, so it will be no sin for them to work on that day. I have great hopes they'll be able to help her."

When Amos had gone, Naftali covered his face with his hands, hiding tears. "Do *you* think it's Tamar's punishment, inflicted on the child?"

"For myself I don't know, but Tamar sees the child as a gift from the Lord; she sees only perfection in her. She loves her so much! All day she cradles her, sings to her, delights in her. The house is full of laughter. Tamar's like a mother tiger protecting her young, and no matter how many more offspring she may have, this one will always be her special favourite. She calls her Avionah, flower of desire."

Recalling the Avionah, beautiful only at night, Naftali rocked back and fore, mourning his sightless blossom. "Tamar can never have another child," he groaned, "Who will marry a woman with a child born out of wedlock?"

Tamar's child is a princess of Israel, and not outside the Law. We changed the circumstances of the birth!" Joseph beamed.

"I don't understand. What do you mean?"

"The night before we left for Joppa, I went to pray in the House of Prayer in the Upper City. The one where the family of Manasseh prays."

Naftali stared at him in disbelief. "Are you mad, Joseph? What did…"

"Just listen if you can, and I'll explain. I knew Ephraim loved Tamar. Hadn't he sworn the child was his in order to save her? He would have married her, even carrying another's child. So I stood next to him at prayer, and instead of praying, for which I hope the Lord will forgive me, I told Ephraim of my plan to rescue Tamar."

Naftali gasped. "Right under the nose of his father?"

"Not exactly! He had his back to us."

"And then?"

"Ephraim wept with relief. I knew he would! Even before the prayer was over, he asked could he come with us to Greece. It was just what I'd hoped for. I managed to whisper where to meet, and slipped out quickly without his father noticing me."

"Wonderful!"

"Yes. The next day, there he was, outside the Western Gate. Trembling with the fear of discovery, but unspeakably glad to see Tamar.

"And Tamar?"

"Was as glad to see him. She's been fond of him ever since he gave her the cat. And that cat nearly ruined everything, I can tell you Naftali. Jumped out of the basket at the harbour, and we nearly had to abandon her there. Tamar and Abishag wailed so loud, I was afraid we'd be discovered. Eventually Ephraim caught her. He's not stupid, that young man. He'd brought Tamar's bride-price with him, filched it out of the family coffers. Some of it we used to bribe a priest to marry them quickly, just before the ship sailed. What do you say to that Naftali?"

"It's amazing. Tamar with a child and a husband. Does Ephraim love my... love the child?"

"Like his own. In time I think you'll be happy for them. They're a real family now, and Abishag adores the baby. She will be her eyes. A blessed girl, more like a sister than a servant. Tamar is talking of finding her a husband amongst the Greeks."

"I'm already happy for them, Joseph, truly. When Tamar and I parted, I felt great love for her, but it was the love of a brother for his sister, not passion or desire. It's Father that I feel for. Rachel is ill, though not so mad as Father thinks; her suspicions aren't all madness as you know. But what chance has she to recover while I'm under the same roof? Now I've seen you, and know Tamar is safe, I feel I should leave home for Rachel's sake and my own. I'm desperate to find peace."

"Where would you go?"

Naftali lay back, eyes closed, and went on talking wearily. "While I was in Egypt, staying with the Essenes, for a brief but unforgettable hour, I truly experienced the real meaning of peace and blessings. If only I could regain even a glimpse of it. I'm ready to go anywhere, into the wilderness even, to find it. I feel like a dried-out well, Joseph, clogged up with stones, and any water of love and blessing is buried deep underneath."

"Wells can be cleared. You liked the Essene way of life? Go to Qumran, find help there. But before that, you'll need to tell Amos the truth about Tamar."

"I've wanted to for a long time, the deceit is gnawing at my very soul. But is it right to tell him? Tamar and I have already caused him so much pain. Wouldn't it be wrong to add to it by confessing? How can I do that?"

"Amos is no fool, Naftali. He probably knows or suspects already…Tell him. It won't kill him, he's a strong man. Tell him, and start afresh."

"Joseph the soothsayer. How am I to thank you?"

Joseph's kind brown eyes beamed. "Will you come to our house tonight? Sarah wants to see you."

"Sarah hates me."

"No. She's always loved you. She was angry because of Tamar. Women are always so keen to blame the man. Now Tamar is safe and well, Sarah is asking after you, and I think she'll tell you she missed your company, and wants to be your friend again. So please come."

"I'll come," Naftali said, moving to embrace his friend.

* * * * *

Naftali and Amos were up and bathed long before the ram's horn ushered in the Day of Atonement. Dressed in white, barefoot and fasting they joined the throng converging on the Temple.

Under dark clouds which promised an early rain, the penitents prayed for forgiveness. As the priests enumerated each sin, Naftali was acutely aware of the Recording Angel hearing the confessions. To cover his fault would be to forfeit inscription in the Book of Life. He had at last confessed to God in prayer, but had yet to tell his father.

"For the sin of breaking the commandments," intoned the priests. Naftali struck his breast. How can I tell him? I can't add to his pain. Must I add to his pain? "Oh Most Merciful have mercy" he groaned, responding with the congregation.

The priests continued the litany, enumerating all the sins of Israel, until they reached the most awful "For the sins for which we are liable to the penalty of death by the hand of Heaven."

"Oh Most Merciful have mercy," the people pleaded as one. 'My sin was punishable by a most dreadful fiery death Naftali thought, and yet here I stand, one of the living dead, an outcast from forgiveness. Amos was looking at him meaningfully. Could it be he already knew?

An expectant hush fell on the crowd. The high priest, dressed in special robes, a rope around his ankle, came up the steps that lead to the Holy of Holies. He was going in. Would he be struck down by Divine Wrath? The crowd held its breath. Would the Lord accept the atonement offered in the name of the people? No one but the High Priest was fit to enter the Sanctuary where the Spirit of the Lord dwelt. If the priest failed to reappear, they would drag his body out by the rope around the ankle. A collective sigh of relief as he came out, only to go back in again. Twice more he went in, and then it was done. The Lord would forgive His nation.

Laying his hand on the scapegoat, the priest transferred all the sins to the wretched animal. The goat's eyes rolled in terror as it was lead away to be hurled from a ravine in the wilderness, where it would perish together with the sins of Israel.

Silver trumpets sounded a triumphant note to the sky. All sins were forgiven! Let the rejoicing start!

"Father, I want to tell you something," Naftali said.

All around them people pushed past, eager for home, and the feast to celebrate their inscription in the Book of Life; but father and son stood in silence, as Naftali searched for words.

Soon the Outer Court was deserted, save for a few attendants.

"I'm going to leave our home, father."

Amos didn't reply, and Naftali struggled on, "Father, there is truth in what Rachel says about Tamar and I."

"I've thought it for a long time."

"You said nothing."

"I was waiting for you to tell me, to ask for forgiveness. I kept on hoping it wasn't true. Can you tell me even now it isn't true?"

"The child is mine, father, the sin is mine. Can you ever forgive me?"

"Can you forgive yourself? When I first suspected, I was so angry that I wanted to hand you to the Sanhedrin. But how can a father condemn his son? My daughter was already condemned to death; should I kill my son too? Bitterness ate at me like a worm. There were times when I wanted to strike you, when I couldn't look at your face. I thought, if I forgive him, this bitterness will pass. I tried to forgive in my heart, but still the worm twisted inside. I prayed and prayed for deliverance, and today at last the Most High showed mercy. Such compassion! The bitterness drained out. Now there is an emptiness, but at least I can bear to look at you again. Be at peace, Naftali, it's forgiven."

Naftali's face showed his disbelief.

"It's forgiven," his father repeated.

"Your forgiveness shames me."

"Not *my* forgiveness, the forgiveness of the Most High," Amos said, opening his arms.

As father and son embraced in the deserted courtyard of the Temple, a heavy rain started, mingling with their tears.

"It's a sign of blessing," Amos said softly, looking skywards, holding cupped hands to the rain.

Chapter Twenty Two

The Gift

Rachamim's heart sang as he walked to the pottery The night with Shulamith had at last been blessed by the Angel of Joy, the morning graced by her smile as she passed, greeting him by name. Never had his name sounded so sweet. And her smile! The merest flicker of long lashes, the curve of the wide mouth before she rounded the wall leading to the southern reservoir, carrying a pitcher.

Turning to watch her pass, his eye was caught by something glinting on the sun, and he went over to see what it could be. There was no mistaking the chalice, its very fragments were graceful. Thoughtfully, he picked them up , and went into the pottery, where he was met by a troubled Dinah.

"Rachamim, Yedidyah is distraught, and he won't tell me why. This morning he didn't go to school, he just sat, didn't speak, didn't even eat, though I baked special bread just for him. He's been like this since yesterday. He won't tell me what's wrong, so I thought perhaps you could talk to him. Maybe he'll speak to you."

Rachamim opened his hands, showing her the shards. "See for yourself Dinah. He broke the chalice."

"Not the one he's talked about endlessly for weeks, the one Nathan glazed for him?"

"The same."

"Can't it be mended?"

"Perhaps Nathan can do it. I certainly can't." He laid the pieces carefully on Nathan's work bench. "I'll come and see Yedidyah after I've finished my work."

"No. Please come now, . I can't bear to see him like this."

"I'll ask Nathan."

"Ask Nathan what?" Nathan said coming in.

"Will you allow Rachamim to come and see Yedidyah?" Dinah asked.

"The cup broke," Rachamim explained.

Nathan fingered the fragments. "I can't possibly mend it, there are far too many pieces, but Yedidyah is welcome to come and make another chalice. Go and tell him now, he must be feeling so miserable."

Rachamim and Dinah hurried to her home, only to find it empty.

"He's probably gone to school," Dinah said relieved, "at least he's taken the bread. Will you go and see if he's there?"

But when Rachamim reached the awning which sheltered the pupils, no one had seen Yedidyah, and a search through the Scriptorium and the kitchen proved equally fruitless.

Where shall I look, Rachamim wondered with a jolt of alarm. In the extreme heat of the desert, a child would quickly perish for lack of water. Shading his eyes, he swiftly scanned the surrounding cliffs. Ah, the cave. That's where he would be hiding.

Glad of his short brown working tunic which allowed him freedom of movement, Rachamim climbed the cliffside as quickly as he could, dislodging showers of stones in his haste. The cave was cool and dark, but held nothing except a few useless jars left by the scribes. He sat down to rest, pulling thirstily at his full water-skin. Yedidyah had comforted him in this very cave, and now the boy was in need of comfort himself, wherever he was.

Slithering down the steep cliff side, he suspected Yedidyah might be with Menachem in the House of the Sick. Why hadn't he thought of it earlier, before this wasted climb?

But the House of the Sick was empty, except for Amnon, huddled on a bed, disconsolate. He started up as soon as he saw Rachamim.

"I didn't mean to frighten the boy. Menachem told me not to go beyond the enclosure, but I needed water. I looked over the wall to find the cistern."

"Which boy are you talking about?" Rachamim demanded with a sinking heart. "Was it Yedidyah? Did you say anything to Yedidyah?"

"No. I said nothing. He ran off. He had something in his hand. He threw it down and ran."

"Where's Menachem? Did you tell him this?"

Amnon shook his head, ashamed. "Menachem's not here today. Yesterday I was afraid to tell him, and this morning when I wanted to explain, he'd already left for Jerusalem. Will you speak to Yedidyah for me, to say I meant no harm? I'm so sorry, so very sorry I frightened the boy."

"I've got to go," Rachamim said.

After a hasty meeting in the Council, it was decided. The search started immediately after the noon meal. All but the oldest members left the Settlement, fanning out in every direction, under the merciless glare of the sun. One by one they returned at nightfall, dispirited and sad. It had been a fruitless search.

146

Rachamim was the last to come back. One look at the face of the watchman, and he knew Yedidyah was still lost.

"They want you to go to Bet-Zayit," the watchman said, "to see if he went home. You were chosen as you've been there before, and know exactly where he lives. You can take a donkey, and Ezra is prepared to go with you if you need him."

"Ezra must be tired, I'll go alone," Rachamim said; a decision he was later to regret.

Heedless of his own fatigue, not stopping to bathe or eat, he hurried to the north gate, where a strong young donkey was waiting, laden with food and water for his journey. Grasping the halter, he was about to mount when he heard light footsteps behind him. It was Shulamith.

"This is for you," she said shyly, placing a cloth bundle into his hand. The warm brown fingers brushed his for a brief moment, her eyes tender in the moonlight.

She walked away, and Rachamim untied the cloth with hands that trembled. Inside was a small jar, suspended on a thong. Pulling out the stopper, he found it contained a salve, bitter-sweet with the scent of myrrh. He slipped it round his neck, burying his face in the cloth, inhaling its fragrance.

Then he wound the cloth round his head, spoke the prayer for the traveller, and set off, heading north towards Bet-Zayit.

* * * * *

With only one more day to go before the Festival of Succoth, Leah was putting the finishing touches to her booth. Reaching up to the latticed roof, she hung a bunch of grapes, green as glass, and stepped back to admire her handiwork. Beside her, on a folded blanket, her baby son Shaul slept peacefully.

Shoshana came rushing in, "Imi, Imi, it's Yedidyah. Yedidyah came back Mother."

Then he was there, hugging her, "Imi, shalom, I've come home."

He was taller, she noticed, his hair bleached by the sun, brown face streaked with dust and sweat.

"Yedidyah! How did you come? Who brought you?"

"I came alone," he looked at the ground, unwilling to meet her eyes. "They don't know I'm here."

"Alone!" she gasped, "You walked at night? They don't know you're here? Tell me what happened. Why did you run away?"

"I'd made a cup, Mother," Yedidyah began, starting to cry.

Leah took her son by the hand. "Come, sit down, tell me slowly, from the start, so I can understand what you say. What cup child?"

"He came there, Mother, Amnon came to Qumran, and I was so angry I threw the cup down and it broke. It took so long to make, and now I've smashed it." He blinked back tears.

"What was Amnon doing in Qumran? Tell me exactly what happened. Did he hurt you?" She clutched him fiercely.

Impatiently, Yedidyah disentangled himself. "No, he didn't hurt me, I was just angry. I never wanted to see him again, and there he was in Qumran. He's spoiled Qumran for me, because if he's there, I can't stay. That's why I ran away."

Bit by bit, she pieced the story together. "They'll be very worried Yedidyah. They'll be looking for you. Why didn't you tell someone? They'd have brought you here."

"I didn't think of that, I just ran. Now I need water. My feet hurt, and my nose from the sun. Father's going to be angry with me, isn't he?"

But once Avinoam had recovered from the shock of Yedidyah's hasty flight, he wasn't angry with his son, he was angry with the Brothers. "They should never have let Amnon come there. If he ever comes back here, I'll beat him and leave him for dead."

"No!" screamed Yedidyah. I did that to him already. It was horrible. All the blood. I dreamed about it so often. All I want is for Amnon to go away from Qumran, so I can go back there in peace."

"You'll not go back there, Yedidyah," Leah said. "If you remember, I never wanted you to go at all. These people harbour evil-doers, they allow children to walk where they please at night, they teach nothing you could not learn here at home. There's a new teacher in the village, and here you stay."

"Mother, I must go back, I must. I made a friend among the pupils, my first real friend, a black boy, black all over. And Rachamim says that now I can read and write, it won't be long before I'm allowed to learn to heal. The teacher in the village can't teach me that. You've got to let me go back."

"Not if Amnon's there," Avinoam said, his tone brooking no argument.

Shoshana brought water. "I'll wash your feet, Yedidyah, they're filthy."

"Can you get this thorn out, Shoshana, it really hurts."

She peered at his foot. "I can't see a thorn."

"I pulled it out, but a piece seems to be still inside. Can you see it?"

She nodded , busying herself with his feet.

"Where's Sheleg?"

"I'll get him when I've finished with your thorn. You haven't even looked at our baby brother. Don't you want to hold him? And there's Ruhama too. Shall I call her? She's to be betrothed soon, but we can still play together. We can do the thanking ritual again."

"I don't feel like doing anything now. I can see Ruhama later. But will you please go and get Sheleg?"

"He'll eat the decorations."

"Not if I tell him not to. Shoshana, do get him for me."

Leah came in with plates of food, but Yedidyah ate little.

"My throat hurts," he explained.

"It's no wonder," Leah said, "all that walking in the dark. Now you must sleep, and then you'll feel better."

* * * * *

Yedidyah was still asleep the next morning when an exhausted Rachamim at last stepped into the welcome shade of the booth, his anxiety turning to relief at the sight of the sleeping boy.

Leah greeted him warmly, hurrying to bring water to wash the hot and dusty feet, calling to Avinoam to come and see their guest.

Avinoam lost no time in greetings. Questions and recriminations tumbled out in a rush. "How could you let the boy out alone? And why did Amnon come to Qumran if not to harm the child? How could you admit such a despicable man? I thought it was a holy place, for prayer and healing, not a refuge for filth."

"No one who comes to Qumran is turned away. Most don't stay long, but those who are not sick, those who come for penance and prayer are expected to work and study. There are no distractions in Qumran. I don't know why Amnon came there, but if he doesn't abide by the rules, he will soon be asked to leave."

"Get him out of there, otherwise I will not allow Yedidyah to return."

"What would you do if Amnon came back to his father's house?"

"First let him come, then we'll see what I will do. A severe beating to start with, and then, if he so much as looks at a child, I swear we'll stone him out of the village."

Rachamim sat down heavily next to Yedidyah, who didn't stir. "Amnon will have to take his chances," he said.

"We'll talk about it later," said Avinoam, suddenly ashamed of the poor welcome to this guest. "You must be tired. Rest here, and I'll see to the donkey. Have you enough water?"

"I've enough provisions for myself and your family as well," Rachamim said, and stretched out thankfully on the ground, fingers straying to the jar around his neck before he fell into a sound sleep.

Moonlight filtered through the leafy roof, the night air was cool. Yedidyah looked around contentedly. A pretty booth. Rachamim the beloved had come and brought peace. He'd said Yedidyah could stay at home for the entire week of the Festival, and after that, Reuven could bring him to Qumran. There would be no Amnon there, Rachamim had promised. His father wasn't going to kill Amnon, though he'd made no promises not to thrash him, and who knew what the other villagers might do? Yedidyah didn't want to think about Amnon.

What a Festival it would be! The olive crop had been good, so there was reason to rejoice, and on the last day there would be a procession with pipes and tambourines, with everyone dancing and singing praises of the Law. Eight whole days to run in the hills with Sheleg, eight days to make another cup in his father's pottery, eight days to talk to Ruhama, and play with Shoshana and the baby. He needn't wash, needn't study, for eight whole days. If only his head would stop hurting.

Shoshana was up at dawn. "Let's go and surprise Ruhama," she said, "Let's ask her to come and see Rachamim before he has to go back."

"My head hurts," Yedidyah complained. "Where's Rachamim? Can you get him?"

Shoshana ran into the house to rouse her mother. She'd seen Rachamim at prayer, and didn't want to disturb him.

Leah laid a hand on Yedidyah's forehead. "I'll bring Rachamim," she said.

"Rachamim," Yedidyah moaned, "My foot hurts."

"He said that yesterday," Shoshana said, "I couldn't see anything."

Rachamim examined the foot. It was red and slightly swollen, but there was no sign of infection.

"It will soon be better. I'll put salve on it, and it will pass." He unscrewed the little jar, thankful to have it. Why hadn't he brought

Ezra with him? Now there was no one to go to Qumran and reassure them the boy had been found. He certainly couldn't go himself, not until Yedidyah was well.

"My head hurts too," the child added plaintively.

"You started walking in the hottest part of the day, so it's no wonder your head aches. That too will go away"

But it didn't, and by the evening, Yedidyah was shaking with fever.

"I've brought no medicines with me," Rachamim told Leah. "Is there anyone in the village who has herbs for a fever?"

"Miriam has," Leah said, sending Shoshana to fetch her.

"Thank the Lord you are here, Brother Rachamim," Miriam smiled. "We can give herbs, and then you can heal him, like you did before."

But Miriam's cooling herbs had no effect. Throughout a night made heavy with fear, Rachamim relived his own impotence in the face of Menachem's sickness. What if he should fail now?

Falling into a tormented sleep, he was jerked awake by the sound of Yedidyah's moan of pain. He stared at him in horror. Yedidyah's face was flushed, his voice hoarse, he could no longer sit. He pointed feebly to his neck, grimacing with the effort, whispering that it hurt, and could Rachamim please make it better very quickly.

I must think of something, Rachamim said to himself; anything.

Leah was asleep in the house, and he went to wake her. "Mother, send Reuven to Qumran. We need healers for Yedidyah. Reuven must go immediately, and hurry."

Leah plucked nervously at the fringes on her shawl. "He'll go, but can't *you* do something? What is this sickness? You healed him before when he broke his foot. Why can't you help him now?"

Getting no response from Rachamim, she cried, "You've got to help him." Then she rushed to the house where Reuven lived with his new wife, calling his name urgently even before she got to his door.

Yedidyah, moaning pitifully, was seized by a spasm in the abdomen, and Rachamim shuddered. He'd seen this illness before, seen how it killed. Patients became stiffer and stiffer until they couldn't breathe, dying open-mouthed in hideous agonies. The dreadful memory of his failure to heal Menachem paralysed him. "I'll give him more medicine," he muttered, knowing it was useless."

The family crowded silently into the booth whose gay decorations mocked their grief. Leah sat rigid, clutching her infant, while Avinoam clasped and unclasped work-worn hands, and Shoshana wept quietly in Ruhama's arms.

At last, Avinoam could bear it no longer. "Do something, Brother," he burst out, thrusting his face into Rachamim's. "Heal our boy. Oh God, please listen. Make him heal our boy. How can he sit there and do nothing? Oh Lord of Compassion, oh Lord of Compassion." He paced in the cramped booth, tears running unchecked down his cheeks.

With a supreme effort, Rachamim gathered Yedidyah's burning body in arms that trembled.

"Leave us alone," he said, "Go into the house and pray. Above all, pray."

Alone with the child, the words of the invocation forgotten, he cried in desperation to the Angel of Healing. Yedidyah's struggles were feebler now. Was the Angel deaf? Or was that thieving Angel of Death even now coming closer to claim the boy? Grimly determined not to surrender this child without a fight, Rachamim would defy the Angel. He laid the tortured body on the crumpled mat, sat down protectively beside him, and closed his eyes.

Stretching his hands out over the boy, he began breathing deeply, stilling his mind, until he was unaware of anything except his breath. With the in-breath, he drew energy from the very depths of the Earth, with the out-breath, from the Sky. Coming to rest in the space between the breaths, Rachamim merged into the great Silence, and in that merging was peace. Infinitely tender was the Angel of Peace as she spread Her deep mantle round man and boy, wrapping them in gentle wings.

Rachamim opened his eyes. Yedidyah's blue ones, wide with wonder, gazed into his, the young limbs were relaxed, the voice soft and low as if he feared to break the silence. "I'll sleep now," he said, reaching up to stroke the cheek of the beloved.

Rachamim continued sitting quietly until tears of gratitude for the gift of healing had ceased to flow. Then he went out to the waiting family.

Raising his arms to the sky in thanksgiving, he said, "The Lord heard our prayers. He is greatly to be praised."

Chapter Twenty Three

A Stony Well

The Succah in Amos' house, though large, lacked the festive touch of former years. Abigail had done her best, but her efforts fell short of the dramatic effects created in the past by Rachel and Tamar. However, the presence of Menachem and Nissim lent an austere peace to the first meal under the palm-frond roof.

"Your wife will recover," Menachem assured Amos, "you've seen how much calmer she is already. Nissim and I will be staying in Jerusalem until the end of the Festival, and when we leave, Naftali will come with us as planned. Until then, take care not to let Rachel see him. It could delay her healing. When she's better, you should take her to Greece, to be with Tamar and her husband and child. Seeing her daughter with a happy life of her own will do more for Rachel than we can do."

Amos turned to Naftali, "It must be clear to you that it pains me to say this, it's something I should have told you before, but I was waiting for it to come from you." He paused, avoiding Naftali's eyes. "I feel the sight of you under the roof will cause Rachel to relapse. I'm forced to ask you to go today, Naftali, before she's is strong enough to leave her room and find you here."

"I'll leave tonight, Father," Naftali said. "What if I am not permitted to stay in Qumran?" he asked Menachem.

"I don't know, only the Guardian can decide."

"Do many seek admittance there?"

"Very few. The climate is so harsh, the monastic life structured and disciplined."

"I want to do penance. Could that bring forgiveness and peace?"

"Again I don't know, but I can tell you that for those who have made Qumran their home, there is no more rewarding way of life."

"What if he's not accepted?" Amos asked.

"Best wait and see."

"My son will not go empty handed."

"Father, how can I take any more from you? Your gift of forgiveness is more than I deserve." Naftali said.

"The gift is not for you, but for the Settlement." He turned to Menachem. "Levana can be used to benefit the community, so please accept the mare with my blessings. She's an Arabian horse, bred to survive in desert climates, and she'll serve the Community well."

"I'll go now father," Naftali interrupted, "and wait for the Brothers at Joseph's house. Will you give me your blessing before I leave?"

"First there is peace to be made with Rachel," Menachem said gently, gesturing towards the entrance.

Supported by Abigail and Yael, Rachel stood, swaying slightly, in the doorway. Her hair had been neatly braided and covered by a purple veil, and a decent gown hung on her emaciated frame.

As Amos hurried to her side, Naftali paled and got to his feet, but before he could make his escape, Rachel pointed one finger at him. "You," she began, her voice strangely calm.

"He's leaving the house now," Amos said.

"Why should he leave the house?" Rachel asked coldly. "We will leave the house, Amos, you and I. Let Naftali stay here alone, and remember how it was when he had a mother…a sister…a father."

"Mother Rachel, come and sit down," Menachem soothed. "Take some of this date syrup we brought from Qumran. None could be sweeter."

"I thank you," Rachel said, unexpectedly meek, seating herself and accepting the proffered cup.

Naftali again tried to make his escape, but Menachem stopped him. "Wait."

Like a trusting child, Rachel said, "My headache has quite gone Amos. Will you give me some food?"

"The bread carries special blessings," Nissim said.

"I can believe that," Amos' voice was soft with the wonder of Rachel's return to sanity.

Rachel ate slowly, seemingly unaware of Naftali's continuing presence. "I'm tired Amos," she said finally. "I'd like to go to my room. Will you bless me Brother, before I sleep?"

Menachem prayed raising his hands over her head, "May the Lord lift up the light of His Countenance upon you, and be gracious unto you. May He give you His peace."

Rachel smiled.

When she'd been taken to her room, Amos said, "What I can't understand is the speed of her recovery."

"Nissim can explain," Menachem said.

"Healing can come quickly, like the rain," the herbalist began, his earnest peasant face crinkling as he searched for words. "After rain, green things grow, even in a desert."

"My wife is no desert, and what are these green things you talk of?"

Nissim, lost for words, looked to Menachem for help, but Menachem ignored him, and he was obliged to continue. "Sometimes a man or a woman is like a desert because love has dried up in their heart," he said.

That's just how I feel, thought Naftali, a dried up well, full of stones. "So how does the desert get to bloom again?" he asked hopefully.

"First the Angel of Healing pulls up the weeds."

"Weeds?"

Nissim shook his head. "Menachem can explain it better."

"Hatred is like a weed," Menachem said, "and when it's pulled up, there's room for the flower of forgiveness to grow."

"And flowers need water," the gardener finished triumphantly. That water is from the Angel of Love."

"Flowers...desert...weeds," Amos questioned, "I don't understand. Did you understand, Naftali?"

"The desert is a heart barren of love, the weeds are hatred, the water love, the flower forgiveness," Naftali said. "Isn't that what you meant Nissim?"

"I think so," Nissim said gratefully.

Chapter Twenty Four

Penance

Menachem rode ahead on the beautiful white horse, while Nissim and Naftali walked leading the donkey laden with gifts from a grateful Amos. As they descended the winding trail, Nissim drew stones from the well of Naftali's loneliness, but not with words. He walked in silence, allowing Naftali to view the wilderness through his own quick eyes. As they came to a ravine, whose cliffs soared golden into the sky, he tugged at Naftali's robe, brown finger pointing. A herd of horned ibex stood immobile, huge eyed, watching them pass. Nissim drew Naftali's attention to a tiny dormouse with pointed snout and miniature ears, warned him wordlessly of the coiled snake, basking in the sun, painted markings echoing the stones. No beauty of Nature seemed to escape the notice of this Brother, who shared his wonder at the very tiniest of leaves sprouting after rain, the new green of a solitary acacia.

As the day drew to a close, lengthening shadows turned cliff and dune to rose and gold. The sun's glowing disc, curtained by filmy cloud spread radiance over the still waters of the sea. They were nearing Qumran, and when at last they came in sight of it, and heard the songs of praise rising in the pure air, a sweetness rose in Naftali's heart. The stony well had begun to fill, and he walked weeping through the gate.

* * * * *

"Yedidyah ben Avinoam, why are you talking? You no sooner get back to your studies than you start disrupting the class."

"I'm sorry, teacher Malkiel," Yedidyah said, arranging his features in what he hoped was an appropriate display of remorse.

But Malkiel was not to be fooled. "After school, you will stay back and copy a psalm of David."

Not a long one, I hope, Yedidyah thought. Now there would be scant time to visit the cattle pen. Someone had come and brought a horse to the settlement, and Yedidyah burned to see it. He had seen horses before, on rare visits to Jerusalem, but had not been close enough to touch one. Avinoam had seen to that!

Never had Yedidyah written more carefully. Knowing his work would be rejected if not perfect, he laboured over the tablet, head bent low, sidelocks firmly in his mouth, out of the way. When he'd scratched the words, 'Teach me to do Thy will,' three times in the unfamiliar Hebrew script, he held it up for Malkiel to see.

"It's well written," Malkiel pronounced, dismissing him, "Remember what you wrote, and learn it."

Yedidyah's friend Hillel had waited for him, and together they walked, chattering like parrots, to the cattle-pen. But it was closed. Strongly constructed of wooden uprights laced with palm fronds, it offered mere chinks for the inquiring eyes of the two friends.

"I can see nothing," Hillel exclaimed, trying to part the fronds with his hands, "We'll have to climb."

Yedidyah looked doubtful. "I've been writing, 'Teach me to do Thy will.'"

"I haven't," said Hillel. His strong hands gripped the uprights through the palm fronds, black legs flashing under the yellow tunic as he reached the flimsy roofing, and peered beneath it.

"Come on Yedidyah, it's easy. Just wait until you see the horse. Come on, it's a beautiful mare."

If I can climb the fence, it must be the Lord's will that I see that horse today, Yedidyah reasoned. Hadn't Malkiel himself taught that nothing could happen which was not the Lord's will?

He was a good deal shorter than the lanky Hillel, the fence was quite high, and the palm fronds sharp, but Yedidyah was determined. Kicking off his sandals, he placed his feet warily in the spaces already cleared by his friend, heaved himself up, slipped through the awning and dropped quietly into the hay on the other side.

That horse was the most wonderful creature he'd ever seen. Yedidyah stroked her gently, savouring the rich horse smell, rubbing his cheek over her soft nose, twining his fingers in the creamy mane. He loved her.

"I'd like to sit on her back," Hillel said bravely.

"Me too, more than anything."

"Someone's coming," Hillel said in a loud whisper, scampering to the far wall and shinning up. "Quick Yedidyah," he hissed, jumping to safety on the outside.

But Yedidyah couldn't risk the scratchy palm fronds again. His feet were already bleeding. He looked desperately for a hiding place, but it was too late. The gate opened, and a young man came in. Long chestnut hair, thick dark brows, striped robe...he looked familiar.

"Teacher Naftali!" Yedidyah yelped, fear turning to delight.

Naftali blinked in surprise. "Yedidyah ben Avinoam. What are you doing here?"

"I live here now. I came to see the horse. What are *you* doing here, Teacher Naftali?"

"I'm not a teacher any more. I came only yesterday. I'm to tend the horse."

"Did you bring her? She's lovely. Can I sit on her? Can I Naftali?"

Naftali lifted the slight body in strong arms, hugging the child to him before swinging him on the horse. "There, how does it feel?"

Yedidyah was gasping with delight. "Will you lead her out?"

"I'm taking her for exercise, but you can ride just a little way. Hold fast to her mane."

"Take me as far as Dinah's house. I must show her."

"Where's Dinah's house?"

Yedidyah pointed.

"A long ride," Naftali said, retrieving Yedidyah's abandoned sandals. "And I'm not sure you deserve it. Look at the fence, I can see gaps where you put your feet when you climbed; it will have to be mended."

"You'll not tell Dinah, please Naftali. I've been in too much trouble lately. If I get in any more, they'll never let me learn to heal...Hillel," he shouted, "Where are you? Come and get on the horse with me! He can, can't he?" he pleaded as the curly-haired Hillel emerged cautiously from behind a boulder.

Naftali smiled. It lifted his spirits to be in the company of children.

* * * * *

Climbing half-way up the cliffside, Naftali sat with his back to a huge rock, and looked out over the settlement. He sat as still as he could, for the hot air clung like an oppressive garment, and any movement intensified his discomfort. He'd been here only eight days now, but it seemed like an eternity. So much had happened since his admission. He'd imagined the Guardian to be old and stern, but he'd been wrong. The deep-set eyes in the youthful face were kind, the expression not without humour. That first day, he'd listened patiently while Naftali told him all the events leading up to his need for penance. Naftali had been honest, keeping nothing back, but the Guardian hadn't laid any penance on him apart from a strict adherence to the monastic life in Qumran. Naftali was welcome to stay for a year's trial period, sharing a tent with others outside the Settlement walls. If at the end of that period he found he wanted to join the Brotherhood, there would be a further three years of trial, leading to possible initiation into the Community. The Guardian's parting words had been interesting, 'As you pluck the stones from the well of your heart, you'll find you have built a Temple there.' How had he known about my stony well? Naftali wondered tiredly.

Work had started immediately, and before the day was over, Naftali knew what the Guardian meant when he'd said no additional penance was necessary; mere survival here was enough. First, a Brother had brought him a short brown tunic, and instructed him in the use of the hatchet carried by the Brothers. The hole must be at least a foot deep, he'd said, and you must be careful not to affront the rays of the sun by revealing your body; keep it hidden by your robe. With such a short garment, this had proved difficult, and Naftali had been forced to walk far into the desert for the relief of needs. He'd tried to control his dismay on hearing excretion was not permitted on the Sabbath, but the Brother had explained how fasting would help.

If that first day had been hard, the subsequent days were even harder. The first day in Qumran had seemed like a year, but the second day had lasted a lifetime. He'd been forced to rise well before dawn after a night spent sleepless on the ground in a stifling tentful of men. Then he'd been instructed to bathe in one of several mikvas, and after putting on his own robe, received his first meditation instructions. Naftali winced, remembering it. He'd been instructed to face east, and greet the Angel of Joy, and this had proved impossible. Not only had he felt no joy, rather, he'd experienced pangs of a remorse so sharp it brought him to bitter tears. His tutor, the patient Phanuel, had seemed to think this was good. "Joy can't come till remorse has gone," he said.

There was no morning meal, but after pulling on the revealing work tunic, Naftali had been expected to sweep the compound. He who had never even touched a broom, had discovered that in the blistering heat of a desert wind, sand and dust fly into every orifice, sting the eyes, invade the mouth and teeth, clog the ears, and set the head to throbbing. No sooner had he swept one paving stone free of sand, than the wind blew the sand back. Even when the wind abated, it was no better, as Brothers returning from work outside the compound left sandy trails, and he had to start afresh. He'd hoped for respite after the noon meal had been served and eaten in austere silence, and had been dismayed to hear that rest was only for the infirm; the blazing afternoons were for work. He'd swept the same paving stones all over again. And then, when others were resting from their work, there was the horse to groom and exercise, and the shed to clean before changing clothes yet again for evening prayers.

The evening contemplations on Peace were harder even than the ones on Joy. How could anyone experience peace, with eyelids stuck together over inflamed eyes, and a belly cramping from hunger as it rebelled against the sparse rations. The days were implacably full. After the meditation, he was expected to study, and learn the unfamiliar chants, croaking the strange liturgy till the signal came for rest. That first dreadful day, he'd have welcomed a visit from the Angel of Death. However was he to raise a Temple of worship in a body so tired he could barely sit upright? Penance was worse than he'd ever conceived, and this was only the beginning.

Chapter Twenty Six

The Visit

Rivka raised her head cautiously and peered at her ankles. It was a miracle! All the swelling had gone, leaving her limbs as slender as a girl's. The medicine had been vile, bitter as worm-wood, but she'd swallowed it, and after a brief time had been forced to ask the attendant to take her to the privy. That young woman had said Rivka was not to walk, the privy would come to her, and she'd brought a vessel right there to the bed. The shame of it! Then the wonder of the damned up flow bursting into the pot. Shulamith had carried it off to empty it, and had brought more medicine, and the whole process had repeated itself. Rivka was ashamed to keep calling her, but Shulamith was all smiles. She seemed to think it wonderful, what was happening to Rivka.

It was all the doing of that rascal Yedidyah. He'd been visiting Bet-Zayit at the time, he'd spied on her as she'd strained over the privy in the courtyard of his mother's house, and he'd guessed; Rivka was drowning in the swelling tide of her own waters. Surely there must be a way to make them come out? He'd begged her to return with him to Qumran, but she'd refused. No strangers were going to poke and prod at her bloated body, she'd rather die.

But when she'd fallen into a fever, her body brown and emitting a foul smell, she'd been too weak to protest. They'd put her in a cart pulled by a white horse, with Yedidyah perched on its back, and Naftali leading it, and brought her to Qumran.

Rivka looked around the House of the Sick. Rachamim, the Brother in charge, was praying for the old man, who appeared to be dying. An attendant fanned the woman on the bed next to hers, and Rivka longed for a little cool air herself, but today her nephew hadn't come to fan her. She loved the stories he told as he fanned. It seemed the young man, Naftali, had just been made one of the teachers at the school. This was interesting, Yedidyah had said, because Naftali had changed. He'd been Yedidyah's teacher before, in Bet-Zayit, when Yedidyah was only a little boy of six, and the lessons had been so dull. Now there was no need to try to enliven them with hairy spiders captured expressly for that purpose. Naftali made the lessons interesting, he made the words of the dullest Scripture come alive. Yedidyah said it made him happy, being with Naftali because Naftali seemed happier himself, almost as if he be were laughing inside. No wonder all the pupils liked him. Naftali was going to stay on in Qumran, so there was no immediate risk of having a boring teacher replace him. Rivka closed her eyes; she was so tired.

Rachamim came over to her side as she slept. He would fan her until Yedidyah came to take over from him. Now that he was in charge of the House of the Sick until Menachem and Nissim returned from Jericho, Rachamim had less time to spend with Shulamith , but tonight he was determined to speak with her.

Yedidyah burst into the room, earning himself a dismissive gesture. Rachamim insisted on silence round the sick at all times, but Yedidyah was undaunted, "Brother Rachamim," he whispered loudly," Menachem and Nissim have returned from Jericho. They're outside, waiting for you."

Quickly Rachamim handed him the fan, and went out.

Yedidyah lost no time in telling Rivka the news. He'd been detained in the school, copying yet another script, and he'd overheard Menachem and Nissim talking to the scribes in the adjoining Scriptorium. Herod the King was dead! Not even Menachem had bccn able to save him It had been awful, Yedidyah reported with relish, there'd been a vile stench, the King's body had swollen with corruption, crawled with worms, and the end had been slow and painful.

Rivka looked at her nephew, so tall, so straight, his strong arm wielding the fan through the stifling air, his shining hair lifting slightly in the breeze he'd created; a boy to be proud of. But what had those mothers of Bet-Lehem got but bitter memories and grieving hearts? She was not sorry the King was dead. "May his name be erased," she prayed. She stayed awake long after Yedidyah had gone to bed, and came to a decision. She would remain in Qumran after she'd recovered, and help in the House of the Sick. Here she could be useful, a help to the community, and here she could see her favourite nephew every day. Forty wasn't too old, her body could still work.

The next day, she waited impatiently for Yedidyah to come, so she could tell him her plan, but he crouched down by her bed to talk, eyes shining with unnatural brightness.

"They're coming back," he told her, "Naftali will go and fetch them, and Shulamith is to go too, to help on the journey."

"Slowly, Yedidyah, who are coming back? What are you talking about?"

"He's coming to visit. I'm going to see him again. Aunt Rivka, it's so wonderful! How long will it take, do you think, for Naftali to bring them?"

"I still don't understand what you're talking about."

"Do you remember the baby from Bet-Lehem, the one who escaped with his parents to Egypt, when Herod tried to kill him?"

"The one you called Immanuel?"

"That one, yes. He's called Yeshua now. Naftali keeps telling me this, but I was there when his mother said, 'He is Immanuel,' and that's what I always call him. Anyway, Immanuel can come back now that Herod's dead and can't harm him."

"They'll come here, you say?"

"They live in Galilee, but will come here first. I asked if I could go too. I'd be helpful. I'd carry Immanuel when his father was tired, I'd play with him and make him laugh, like Shaul laughs when I play with him. But they say I have to stay here, and study, and help in the garden in Shulamith's place. I think I'll burst, just waiting!"

"If Shulamith is going away, I'll be able to stay and take her place. I'm getting stronger day by day. Does that please you, Yedidyah?"

But Yedidyah didn't seem to have heard. His blue eyes wore a far-away look. "I'm going to see Immanuel!" he said rapturously, "I'm going to see Yeshua!"

* * * * *

Rachamim and Shulamith sat side by side in the deserted garden, inhaling the sharp fragrance of the herbs. Mindful of the laws of purity, the pair sat slightly apart from each other, and only the eyes caressed. Love had blossomed as a rose between them; its flowering hedged by thorns.

Although they had come together every month on the permitted day, their coupling had born no fruit, and Rachamim was afraid he would lose his bride if he failed to impregnate her. Marriage could not be sanctioned until Shulamith proved she could bear children, but the strain of this knowledge, and the enervating heat had been too much for Rachamim, who no longer attained union with his betrothed.

"Shulamith," he said, "If we are forbidden to wed according to the rules of the Community, would you leave with me, and be my wife?"

She started slightly. "You would leave Qumran for me? Leave the Brotherhood, and your work with the sick, everything you hold most dear?"

"Shula, everything I hold most dear is right here beside me. Coupling is difficult in the heat of the desert, but in my village on the Plain of Sharon, the winds blow sweetly from the sea, even when the sum is at its height. There you could be fulfilled, and conceive the child you long for. Come with me. My brothers will build you a house, my mother welcome you as a bride, my sisters as one of them. Rose of my heart, you shall stand beside me beneath the marriage canopy, and the Angel of Fertility will bless us with sons."

Shulamith smiled, "But I've grown to love Qumran. And what of our work here?"

"I've thought of that. We would take our work with us. I can continue healing the sick, you can grow the herbs, and prepare the medicines. You shall have a garden more fertile than this, watered by frequent rains. We will make our own little community, and live as we live here, in service and prayer."

"When would we leave?"

"Naturally not until you return from Egypt with the family. Perhaps not even then, as we'd have to wait until Ezra is ready to take my place in the House of the Sick, and Yedidyah to tend the garden in your place."

"I have no dowry, nothing. How can I leave?"

"My father will waive the bride price as soon as he sees your lovely face, and my sisters will make you a dress fit for a Queen of Israel."

She laughed. "Me, a Queen!" She fingered her worn blue skirt. "What colour for my bridal robe?"

"Why blue, of course, and lilies for a crown. I'll fill your arms with roses. Say you'll come with me?"

"There is a colour like the sky at sundown. Do you think it will look well on me?"

"I will think, and let you know!"

But she was to leave for Egypt before he could decide.

* * * * *

"Aunt Rivka, Naftali's been gone ten days now. See, I marked the days on my girdle."

"Is it ten days already? For ten days I've been saying I'll get up and help Rachamim and Noemi, the new attendant, and still this lazy Rivka lies on the bed."

"Tomorrow, Aunt Rivka, when I come, your bed will be empty, you'll be sweeping the courtyard. Why didn't you eat the food Dinah brought? She made it specially for you?"

"I'll eat it later, when the night is cooler."

"The nights will not be cooler now, for the summer is on its way. Look at the moon, how bright it is. Surely it will light the way for Immanuel's coming."

Rivka forced a smile, Her limbs were lighter now, her body slender, yet it still felt so heavy. She must get up and dress herself; she should be helping Noemi, who was no match for the capable Shulamith.

Rivka raised herself on feeble arms, only to fall back exhausted on the bed. What was the matter with her? Why wouldn't her body obey?

Yedidyah watched in silence, and then went to find Rachamim.

"Rachamim, it's been days now, and still Aunt Rivka lies there, very quiet, and she's so thin. She doesn't even speak to me very much any more, just smiles when she sees me coming. She can't get up. Why isn't she better? Can you ask Menachem to heal her?"

Rachamim placed a gentle hand on Yedidyah's shoulder. "Come, let's sit down quietly, I'll explain."

He lead Yedidyah to the wall near the pottery, and they sat side by side, looking out over the distant Sea shining like silk in the moonlight.

Then Rachamim said slowly and carefully, "Sometimes a person's body can't be healed, because it's worn out, and of no further use to the soul living in it. Then it's best not to try to make the body strong, but kinder to leave it in peace, so that the angels can lead the soul away to the heavens."

"Not Aunt Rivka. She isn't old and worn out. She can't die yet; not before she's seen Immanuel. I couldn't bear it if she didn't see him. Besides, she says she wants to live and work here with us. Can't any of you make her better? Please try. Don't let her die."

"We don't know how long it will be before the family of Yeshua comes. Maybe it will be soon if they find a good ship, and the winds are favourable."

"And if we ask the Angel of Death to wait till then? Shall we try? Do you know the words?"

Rachamim shook his head, but Yedidyah was determined. "Then I'll make them up. I want the Angel of Death to wait; I know that if Rivka sees Immanuel, she'll be healed." He shut his eyes tight, screwing up his face in earnest prayer. "Do you hear me Death? Wait, please, don't take Rivka. Listen to me and wait."

Rachamim would have taken the boy in his arms, but Yedidyah was not a child any more. He stood with his legs apart, a fierce young warrior lifting his arms to the sky, wrestling with Death.

* * * * *

Rivka died peacefully in her sleep the night before the visit.

As custom dictated in that hot land, she was buried immediately, far from home and family, in the stony ground outside the settlement. Rivka had endeared herself to those who knew her because of her calm endurance and cheerful spirit, but as everybody in the Settlement was busy with special guests, few came to mourn her. Yedidyah, the only member of her family present, recited the prayer for the dead over the simple grave. He was angry. The Angel of Death had snatched his aunt before the coming of Immanuel, who could have saved her. He hated the Angel. Refusing to eat, and taking only a little water, he sat down disconsolate by the grave, marking it with stones.

Towards evening, Yedidyah's vigil was disturbed by Hillel who came running. "Yedidyah, get up. The watchman on the tower has seen people approaching, with a horse and donkey. It's the family, they're coming! Get up quickly, let's go to the gate. See, I've brought the chalice you made to give Yeshua. I told Dinah, and she's bringing a pitcher with milk to fill it. Get up, please, Yedidyah. Why are you waiting?"

The dream he'd dreamed for so long had been shattered, the longed for moment of reunion with his love snatched away by death. How could he go and leave his aunt alone now? Yedidyah kicked at the ground. "I can't."

Hillel ran off, but returned minutes later with Rachamim.

"Come Yedidyah," Rachamim said gently, "For so long you've waited to greet the family. All the other pupils are at the gate. So stand up and I'll dust you down, as there's no time to change your clothes."

Yedidyah remained seated. Death was a cheat. Immanuel's coming was too late for Rivka, and now it seemed he too had been cheated. The Angel had robbed him of the longed for moment when he'd give the gift to the child, and see him smile. How could he go now to greet the family, feeling so angry, and so sad?

Rachamim coaxed, "Rivka would be angry if you didn't go to greet Yeshua. She'd say what kind of a boy are you, to say you loved the child, and then refuse to welcome him at the gate? Please, Yedidyah, do it for Rivka."

Slowly Yedidyah got up, and Rachamim made a futile attempt to dust down the soiled yellow tunic. Together they went to the gate, and stood with the assembled pupils and some of the elders of the Community.

Dinah had already filled the cup. "Take it, Yedidyah, it's still cool. Give it to the infant when he comes."

Yedidyah shook his head, heavy with disappointment. "No. Hillel can give it. I'm unwashed, and can't give it now. Go on Hillel," he said sadly, retreating to the back of the crowd, where he crouched out of sight behind Rachamim.

Mariam was more beautiful than Yedidyah remembered; serene and smiling, she rode into Qumran on the little donkey, lead by a sun-browned Shulamith. Joseph, carrying the child in his arms, rode the white horse, and behind them came Naftali guiding a woman in a yellow dress.

As Joseph dismounted from the horse, Yedidyah's hungry eyes searched out the child. He was a baby no longer. Sturdy in his little white tunic, shining hair curling round his shoulders, he held his father's hand, looking around fearlessly.

Hillel came forward with the cup, and loosing Joseph's hand, Yeshua walked towards him. Taking the proffered cup, the child drank, then lowered it, searching the crowd over the rim.

He's looking for me, Yedidyah guessed, trembling with excitement. Does he know I love him? That I made the cup for him? Then his Immanuel was coming towards him, threading his way through the people, walking right towards where he was hiding, crouched behind Rachamim. The child halted. Yedidyah could see the sandalled feet planted firmly in the dust. Then Rachamim moved aside, and Yedidyah found himself looking into a pair of shining eyes. Yeshua held out the cup towards him. "Drink."

It seemed to Yedidyah that all the love in the world was in the cup, all the compassion of the Most High, all His tenderness and care. It was everything the boy had ever dreamed of. Waves of light, a timeless sea, broke over him as he drank, filling him so full of unutterable happiness that it found expression in one word only: "Immanuel."

The child smiled. Reaching up, he patted away tears from the boy's face with gentle fingers. Yedidyah got to his feet, and hand in hand the two walked into Qumran.

Glossary

Adar. Hebrew month, February/March.
Bar-Mitzvah. Jewish rite of passage into manhood.
Bet-Lehem. Bethlehem.
Betrothal. Binding promise of marriage.
Bet-Zayit. Fictitious name of village.
Concubine. A secondary wife.
Council of the Pure. Assembly of Brothers at Qumran.
Ellul. Hebrew month, August/September.
Essenes. Jewish sect, probable authors of Dead Sea Scrolls.
Festival of Lights. Modern Hannukah.
Guardian. Leader of Qumran Community.
Hamseen. Hot, dry wind.
Hymns. The hymns are taken from the Dead Sea Scrolls.
Imi. Mother.
Judas Maccabeus. Jewish hero who fought the Greeks.
Kislev. Hebrew month, November/December.
Kyphi. Egyptian perfume.
Mikvah. Bath for ritual purification.
Malka. Queen.
Nameless One. God.
New Year. Jewish, early autumn.
Passover. Jewish festival of liberation.
Procurator. Roman Governor.
Qumran. Settlement of Essenes on shore of Dead Sea.
Redemption of First-born. Jewish ceremony for male children.
Sanhedrin. Jewish Court of Law.
Sea of Salt. Dead Sea.
Shalom. Hebrew, peace.
Shekinah. Angel of the Lord.
Sivan. Hebrew month, May/June.
Wadi. Watercourse.
Yom Kippur. Jewish Day of Atonement.
Zealot. Jewish freedom fighter.